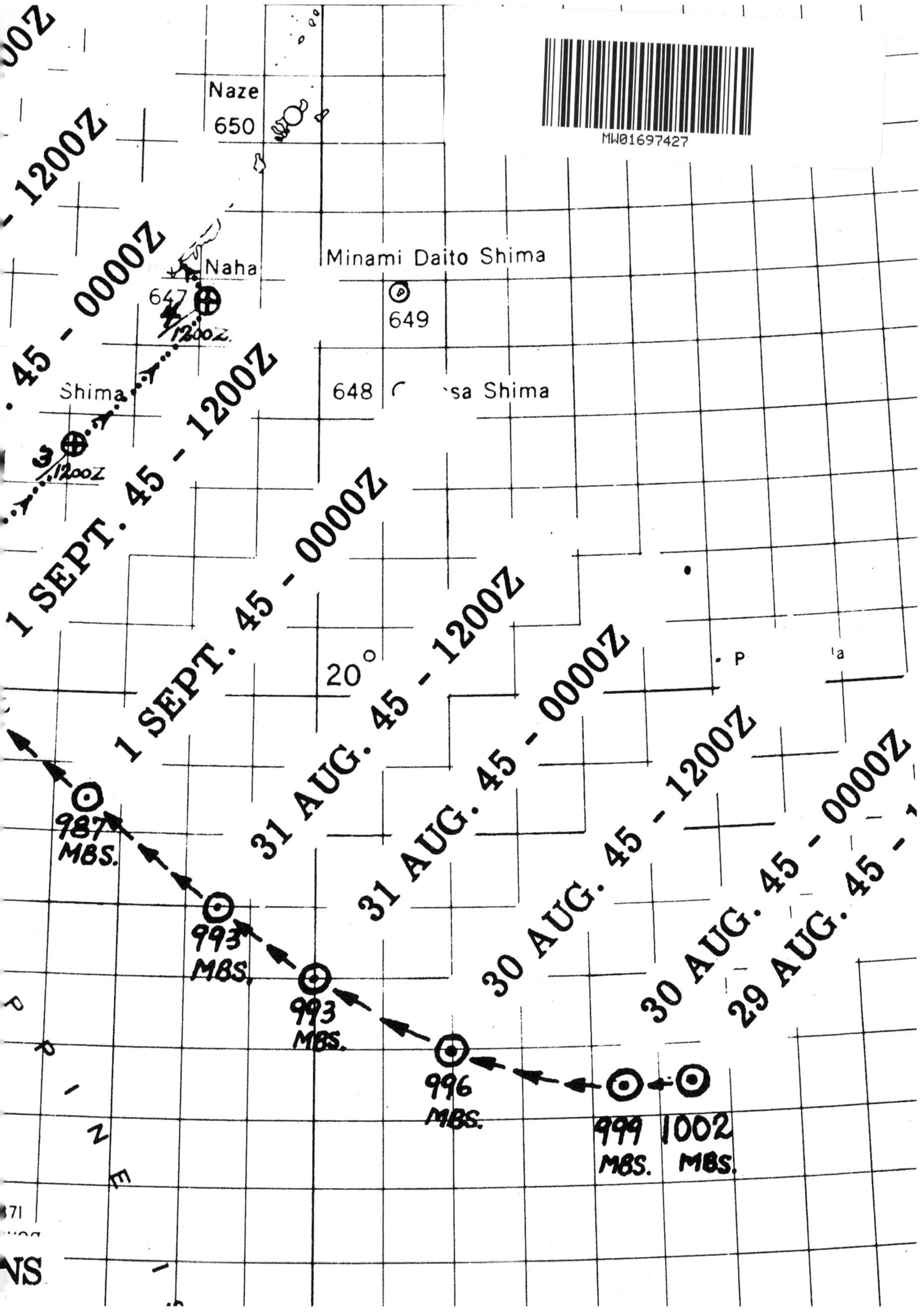

00Z
1200Z
45 - 0000Z
Naze
650
Naha
647
1200Z
Minami Daito Shima
649
Shima
45 - 1200Z
1200Z
648
sa Shima
1 SEPT. 45 - 1200Z
1 SEPT. 45 - 0000Z
31 AUG. 45 - 1200Z
31 AUG. 45 - 0000Z
30 AUG. 45 - 1200Z
30 AUG. 45 - 0000Z
29 AUG. 45 -
20°
987 MBS.
993 MBS.
993 MBS.
996 MBS.
999 MBS.
1002 MBS.
P R I N E

NS

Unlimited Duty

Unlimited Duty

Jim Ingram

ISBN: 978-1-56852-831-1

Production and design services by Konecky & Konecky, LLC.

Endpapers: Weather maps by Jack Ingram from *Typhoons of the Western Pacific*

Printed in China

Acknowledgments

My warm thanks and grateful appreciation to my family and friends, who shared their factual information about Jack Ingram's uniquely colorful life. In addition, I acknowledge Jack Ingram's small diary that served as a treasure-trove of information that revealed his detailed "Trips and Travels."

I thank Barbara Ingram, Jack Ingram, Sage Ingram, Laura Blaguszewski, Mike Valentino, John Ingram, Karen Horvath, Beverly Klucher, Dale DiSanto, Randall Ackerman, Ed Glantz, Sharon Lilly and Sean Konecky, who read the manuscript and helped to synthesize the history of Jack Ingram.

Aside from navy department and other government military records, I also wish to give particular thanks to the U. S. Naval Institute and National Security Agency, for their organization's contributions to *Unlimited Duty.*

And, I thank my dad, Jack Ingram, who always exhibited common sense leadership traits through his personal stories from humble origins as a boy enduring the depression to serving our country as a navy sailor, WWII navy officer and aerographer (meteorologist), navy hurricane hunter and national security pioneer.

A Tribute from Jack C. Ingram

Unlimited Duty chronicles important moments and lessons taught during my grandfather's life. As his grandson and namesake, I have been fortunate to benefit from his wisdom and vision that has extended through the generations of the Ingram family.

We are privileged that his legacy is recorded and shared for others to learn from his life's high standards and instruction. We are indebted to Jack who invested his life in a worthy cause of helping others at every turn to make life better for us all.

Furthermore, I want to thank my dad for being a farseeing guide through the years by illuminating the leadership character traits of my grandfather.

Jack C. Ingram is the grandson of Commander Jack Ingram.

Table of Contents

Preface 9-14

Chapter One ....Get the Lead Out...14-30

Chapter Two....................Bluejacket 31-44

Chapter Three ....Hindenburg Class..45-56

Chapter Four ....Time to Be an Aerographer.......................57-70

Chapter Five....................Philippines..71-84

Chapter Six ....World War II...85-102

Chapter Seven ....Empire Express: "Fly the Weather"........103-114

Chapter Eight ....The Honorable Maverick 115-118

Chapter Nine..................Aerology and Intelligence........................119-126

Chapter Ten ....Naval Justice 127-132

Chapter Eleven..............From Typhoons to Hurricanes...............133-144

Chapter Twelve.............A Higher Intelligence...............................145-150

Chapter Thirteen ....No Such Agency 151-160

Chapter Fourteen.........Seasoned Sailor 161-182

Chapter Fifteen ....Tireless Patriot 183-190

Chapter Sixteen ....Everyone's Dad...191-200

Chapter Seventeen ....Practical Reflections 201-202

Author's Notes..............Sage Advice...203-207

Afterword by Ken Schmidt 209-212

Young Jack in Portland Oregon -1924

Preface

I have always had deep admiration for my father, Jack Ingram. He was a man of incredible integrity who never wavered in his commitment to family, community, and nation. A pillar in our family during his lifetime, he left us with many fond memories, and he continues to serve as an example for us of how to live fully and honorably. His generosity of spirit and the true interest he showed in others are traits that endeared him to many people, both within the family and beyond.

Professionally, he had a fascinating military career in the then-emerging field of aerography (now meteorology) and later in intelligence—he served his country during more than one pivotal moment in history. When I speak with people who knew Jack, I find that they are particularly surprised and interested to hear about his experiences and accomplishments. In fact, their reactions to the stories I have shared about my father's career are a significant part of what inspired me to write this book.

It has been humbling and inspiring to work on this project, which has been many years in the making. I have valued the process as an opportunity to reflect on the time that I am grateful to have spent with my father. I have carried his many leadership character traits and lessons with me throughout my life, and they have served me well.

While he accomplished a great deal professionally—and I spend a good portion of this book documenting those accomplishments—his family was paramount. You will read about his past in the first chapters, and you will learn that my dad was always interested in stories from his elders. As a young man in Oregon in the mid-1930s, he made friends with an eighty-year-old Spanish-American War veteran as well as others who had been pioneers in the old Wild West. He was always prodding them with questions. Just imagine the stories they had to tell!

When I was young, I had the same sort of curiosity—and that's when I began to gather these stories about my father. He never really talked about his past, especially his war experiences, unless you asked him specific questions. I think he learned not to talk about them because of his high-security-clearance restrictions from the navy and National Security Agency (NSA) classified projects he directed.

Although he was not one to regale everyone with tales from his past, I know he would appreciate his family members, and friends (those he knew and loved, as well as future generations) wanting to learn more about him in the context of understanding their history.

Fortunately, I was afforded the perfect opportunity to ask him plenty of questions. Our family raised beagle hunting dogs out in the country on an eighty-acre property we named Bonnie Glen, about half an hour east of State College, Pennsylvania. Bonnie Glen is a beautiful little glen within Penns Valley; thus, appropriately named "Bonnie Glen." It was perfectly set up to raise beagles with its fields, springs, stream, and mountain forest land. We would stay out there with the beagles in the summer, but during the rest of the year they were on automatic feeders and we would stop by to check in on them when the weather was cold. On very cold nights, we would drive out to Bonnie Glen, just to make sure everything was okay and to feed the beagles hot meals.

On our drives, I would ask my dad all sorts of questions, and he would tell me stories about himself. I remember that he would often connect his stories to morals, telling me what he learned from an experience. He had a real gift for helping me to understand the meaningfulness of his stories, and I have tried to incorporate some of the wisdom he imparted into this book. I have tapped into those stories throughout many moments in my life, and they have saved me a lot of trial and error, giving me strength and insight to make good personal decisions and to help others the same way.

In addition to conversations we had over the years, the information in the book comes from a few other notable sources. One is a small journal named "Trips and Travels" that my grandfather, Earl, gave to him in 1935 when Jack joined the navy; it offers a glimpse into his mind and heart. He would make entries into it periodically, sometimes for everyday matters, and other times for significant events. One such event was the explosion of the *Hindenburg*, which he experienced from underneath the airship as a young sailor on the ground crew holding onto one of its mooring lines. The pocket journal spans 1935 to 1980, and it gives some great insight into his personality, faith, outlook, and lessons learned throughout his lifetime.

With the help of research based on his navy records, and by looking across a vast array of his personal documents and interviews, I was able to confirm and elaborate on several stories related to his early life experiences, military service, and later-year occurrences.

Other family members have also been a great source of information. From sharing documents and images that had been filed or stowed away, to telling (and sometimes writing down) stories of their own, they helped to paint a fuller, more detailed picture.

Living through the hardship of the Great Depression and rising to face the challenge of the Second World War were pivotal in shaping the life and character of not just Jack Ingram but his entire generation. These formative experiences, which encapsulated both the fragility of society and the resilience of the human spirit, set the stage for the way he and my mother navigated life and taught us what was important. They wanted to prepare us for the challenges we might face in the future—instilling in us the value of self-sufficiency and making sure we each pursued a good education—while also helping us to realize the responsibilities we have to our community and the people around us.

As you read about Jack, there are many valuable lessons to take away from the stories I have compiled here about leadership, hard work, perseverance, maintaining a positive attitude, and treating others with dignity. For me, the greatest of these lessons—the biggest takeaway from my dad—is to have a clear moral vision, to always do the right thing when it comes to other people. He truly believed, and showed us by example, that when you take care of everyone else, you will be fine. Armed with this humble attitude, Jack accomplished great things over the course of his life, and we are honored to have his legacy as a part of our family and U.S. history.

Tom Brokaw's book about the World War II generation is boldly titled *The Greatest Generation*. Why is that so bold? Because "greatest" is a tremendous claim that begs proof. Well, that generation did prove it.

The men of Jack Ingram's generation volunteered in droves to defend their country during WWII and they are to be commended for their patriotism in answering their country's call to duty. And one must remember that there already were men of the armed forces manning the ships, planes, and trenches as the winds of war were blowing.

Young Jack Ingram, an enlisted man in the navy, got his "baptism under fire" at sea, on land, and in the air in the western and northern Pacific, and especially in the remote, barren Aleutian Islands, an almost forgotten theater of war during WWII.

Though the Aleutian theater was not well known, Jack's exploits became legendary. He had been tasked by Admiral Chester Nimitz to "Keep them flying!" Trying to get the bravest of men to ignore the abominable weather and fly into its icy jaws was a tough thing to do. It took an unusual leader to inspire the flyers to go up in some of the most inhospitable weather on the planet. Jack's great leadership traits sustained him and many others through many WWII trials.

Jack Ingram's story chronicles his adventures from his time as a teen when he was living on the Rogue River in southern Oregon, panning for gold with his dad, to his early years in the navy as a gunner, boxer, and striker on USS *Pennsylvania*. His practical, can-do attitude and propensity for helping others was later exemplified at Lakehurst

Naval Air Station where he found himself helping dozens of people escape from the burning airship *Hindenburg*.

During his career, Jack would volunteer for duty forecasting and flying the treacherous weather around the Aleutian Islands to bomb Japan during WWII. After the war, his many exploits and achievements included hurricane hunting and top-secret field operational intelligence with the newly formed National Security Agency, or NSA, affectionately known as "No Such Agency"—decades of patriotic service to America.

A true maverick, Jack rose through the ranks from navy enlisted man to a temporary lieutenant line officer during WWII, proving himself of incalculable value. After the war, he was commissioned as a lieutenant and later as a lieutenant commander in the new Limited Duty Officer (LDO) category. Because Jack's skills were anything but "limited," he later was transferred from LDO status into the general line with its unrestricted permanent officer commission. Inevitably, Jack's commanding officers realized that his reservoir of hands-on experiences, leadership capabilities, and diverse responsibilities equaled "unlimited duty," which led to his permanent officer recognition.

Jack was a unique and talented lieutenant commander with an outstanding record, making full use of his formative years of practical application and skill in the new science of aerology (meteorology) and operational intelligence. Jack's dedication, courage, and expertise guided his career into rarified circles, gaining the respect and admiration of high-ranking commanding officers such as Commander Wilbur M. Lockhart; Admiral William Halsey; Admiral Nimitz, commander of the Pacific Fleet during WWII; the Joint Chiefs of Staff during the cold war years; and Admiral Noel Gayler, captain of USS *Ranger* and later, director of the NSA and commander of the Pacific Command.

An exemplary man, Jack was also a devoted father who set an example for his six children with his virtuous character, exceptional service, faith, and leadership abilities. He taught all of us to make the best out of every situation and to always help others to do the same.

If anyone could be characterized as an all-American boy who was an outstanding member of the Greatest Generation, who exhibited great leadership character traits, with an "Unlimited Duty" ethic, it would be Jack Ingram.

Chapter One

Get the Lead Out

The warm promise of spring after a cold and damp Oregon winter permeated the air one March morning in 1935. When seventeen-year-old Jack Ingram was in the U.S. Navy recruiting office in Portland, the promise of an exciting new adventure before him was just as strong.

The stout, fierce-looking chief petty officer addressing him was more than a little intimidating. His dress shirt was blindingly white and starched enough to stand on its own. His navy blue uniform sleeve carried the three yellow stripes and eagle of a chief petty officer 1st class. The yellow hash marks at the bottom denoted his years of service. The man scrutinized the ruggedly built, deeply tanned young man before him. He kept looking up from Jack's application to run his sea-worn eyes over the boy.

While Jack maintained a respectful stance, the petty officer called over another recruiter who was busy at his desk. The two conferred in hushed tones. Then the second man, a seaman 1st class, together with the petty officer, scanned Jack.

Young Ingram was now getting restless and obviously uncomfortable.

In a deep, concerning tone, the petty officer asked, "Son, you sure you are originally from Portland and now living in Galice?"

"Sir?"

Patiently he asked again, "You sure you aren't a Multnomah?"

Jack was startled by the question. "Sir, I'm not a Multnomah."

The two went back to their furtive huddle and kept looking from Jack to his application and then referring back to some official-looking navy publication.

When the seaman went back to his desk, the petty officer said, "You sure look like another Multnomah Indian to me."

"Pardon me, sir?"

"You sure seem like an Indian boy from the reservation!"

Now Jack protested. "No, sir! Sir, I grew up in Portland and now live with my dad on the Rogue River near Galice. I've got a birth certificate at my sister's home in Portland to prove it."

The Petty Officer eyed him and said, "Ok, son, you go get it and come on back."

It is important to understand that during the Depression, the regular army and the regular navy were a refuge for men trying to survive. Native Americans were unfairly discriminated against, and it was a poorly kept secret that some recruiting offices were limiting their enlistments. Later, during WWII, Native American contribution is well documented. The Navajo radio operators, called "Code Talkers," were marines who served with great valor in the war. Their success in befuddling Japanese operations was a major contribution to the war effort.

But in the final analysis, Jack's birth certificate, which showed that he was born on Thursday, March 15, 1917, in Portland, Oregon, prevailed. Later, his excellent grades on the entrance exam, which covered aptitude, command of the English language, and math skills, sealed the deal. Jack Ingram was officially enlisted in the United States Navy. The interesting thing about this interaction is that everyone who knew Jack saw him as an "all-American boy" type. It must have been the deep tan and thin muscular build acquired on the Rogue River that put the navy recruiters on the wrong track.

Jack began his navy career as an apprentice seaman on April 17, 1935, shortly after his eighteenth birthday. He had done all his paperwork and he was ready to take his oath and board a train for three months of boot camp at the other end of the West Coast at the U.S. Naval Recruit Training Center in San Diego. Jack, a tall, blue-eyed, handsome, fit young guy with a curious mind and a head full of ideas sat waiting with the other recruits. He would go far in the navy.

As Jack thought about what boot camp would be like, his thoughts drifted back to when he was eleven years old and was about to face the first major change in his life.

Jack's mother, Mary, had just died, which was traumatic for Jack. Eleven was a very painful age for a child to lose his mother. It was old enough to have learned to love her. Old enough to depend on her. Old enough to look forward to her love and nurturing. And old enough to miss her terribly. But thankfully Earl, as a single parent, was the type of father a boy could lean on, depend on. Even so, Jack had to grow up very fast!

Jack was the youngest of his siblings. He had an older brother, Bill, and an older sister, Mary, who were married and had left home. Earl, unable to care for the boy during summer vacations, had sent him to his maternal grandparents every summer. The Jansen family had a dairy farm near Verboort, outside of Portland in the Willamette Valley. The Jansens were a Catholic Dutch family with eleven healthy kids, which meant there were many cousins and friends for the lonely boy. At the farm Jack learned how to work hard, a mix of man and machine, as was required on a farm. He also acquired a good, solid work ethic.

One cousin, Larry, who was three years younger than Jack, became a close companion. The cousins spent countless hours playing baseball on the farm with the Jansen family and other kids from the neighboring farms. Larry Jansen went on to become a well-known winning pitcher for the New York Giants. Larry was twice an All-Star, winning 122 games; he was inducted into the Oregon Sports Hall of Fame in 1980. He wrote a book called *The Craft of Pitching* in 1977.

Jack remembered his days on the farm fondly. Working on a dairy farm was hard work, and there were no days off with cows to be milked. Jack didn't mind the work, though, and he appreciated the simplicity of life and the feeling of being part of a large, devoted family.

A shrill whistle jolted Jack from his thoughts, followed by an announcement that it was time to board the train. All the recruits gathered their belongings, heaving their heavily loaded duffle bags onto their shoulders. The buzz and excitement of the day was apparent, but so was the apprehension about what was to come.

Jack settled into a seat by the window. From there he could see the station and the familiar Cascade Mountains and characteristic Douglas fir trees of his home state. Resting his head against the window, he felt the sudden jolt as the train lurched forward. The wheels began to roll along the track as the locomotive chugged out of the station, each car of the train being tugged in succession. Jack was oblivious to the young men around him. Memories of an earlier time and another great adventure occupied his mind. At the time, he did not realize that the adventure would be a bonding and growing experience that would shape his entire life.

The previous summer young Jack and his dad, Earl, were sharing an experience that seemed like something straight out of the old West. They were panning for gold! There was at that time, and always has been, a romance about gold, not only in America but throughout the world. It represented beauty. Power. Wealth. Security. It always drew men eager to seek it out.

Two years earlier at the height of the Great Depression, Earl could find no work in any of the many fields he had worked in: farmer, logger, steel worker, dock worker, auto-body man, or mechanic. Boilermaker was his primary trade, although he eagerly accepted other jobs when there was no work. The shipyards had suspended all ship building, and times were getting tougher.

Being a boilermaker was a rough job, not only because it was physically demanding but also because it was dangerous. Earl constructed huge boilers that contained steam to drive everything from a ship to a factory power plant to a furnace for heating a building. The boilers had to be built and tested and, in that process, they could blow up. Many did! Earl was known as a leader of men who had a reputation for getting big construction jobs done safely and ahead of schedule.

But the Depression was on and desperate men all over the country were doing everything from selling apples, plums, and roses on street corners of big cities like Portland, to picking fruit and vegetables in the Willamette Valley. Many were enlisting in the armed forces just to get three square meals a day. For Earl, losses suffered from the stock market crash, looming mortgage payments, utility bills, and inconsistent work made life difficult, but he always had a positive attitude with a smile. Jack pitched in to help the family, but working as a school crossing guard and a life guard certainly was not enough to overcome the financial burdens that the Ingram family endured.

The government had some programs to help, such as the Civilian Conservation Corps (CCC), which involved workers living like conscripts in the woods with strict regulations, under government control, working as a labor battalion. Earl, however, had his fill of logging camps early in life and preferred the freedom of being on his own with his son, beholden to nobody. They were part of a breed of rugged individuals imbued with the American spirit.

With foreclosure looming, Earl decided to leave late one night to avoid a sheriff's delivery of a summons the next morning. A close friend had tipped him off—the sheriff himself. Earl had many friends in town, and thank God the sheriff was one of them.

It was 1933, and Jack was going on sixteen when his dad awakened him in the middle of the night to tell him they were going gold mining. Jack didn't question his father; he just starting packing. They loaded the Ford Model A and home-built flatbed trailer with essentials—old army tent, camping and cooking gear, an ax, shovels, crosscut saws, bamboo fly-fishing rods, guns, and basic food provisions—and set out for the Rogue River in southern Oregon near the California border. They drove all night down the coast into the Siskiyou Mountains and did not arrive at their destination until late the next day. Roads back then were rough and tough going!

This turn of events made life rough for Jack, as he had been happy at Clinton Kelly High School of Commerce, later known locally as "Commerce High." Back in 1931, Jack had won the Gilmore Trophy for his abilities as a school crossing guard, protecting the lives of fellow students during the school year. An Oregonian newspaper article said that it had been difficult to choose an outstanding patrol member out of more than three hundred schoolboy officers around Portland. The article went on to say, "Jack Ingram's work was distinguished by the promptness in which reports were made to the police department of the daily activities." Jack's mastery of writing "briefs" for his superiors had been noted at an early stage in his life!

On June 15, 1932, Jack had won Portland's Rose City American Legion Award of Merit recognizing a high school student with outstanding scholarship, leadership, courage, honor, and service. He was sophomore class president, was on the track team, had achieved the rank of Star Scout, and was doing well in his studies—especially English. In fact, his English teacher told him that he wrote like Zane Grey, a popular Western storyteller and novelist. He had also learned to become a proficient typist, which assisted him in his interest in writing.

All of Jack's traits were highlighted in high school. To become class president, one had to be ambitious and popular. Running track showed that he was an athlete; being a rising Boy Scout indicated his passion for the beautiful forests and waters around Oregon; and his good grades proved he was a scholar. In addition, Jack was not afraid of work, always gravitating toward jobs that kept people safe—crossing guard and life guard.

While in school, he was periodically thrust into the rough-and-tumble men's world of the Portland shipyard with his dad, but nothing would compare to the back-breaking shoveling for gold on the Rogue.

Had he not needed to go to work full time at such a young age and had he completed his high school education, he would have had excellent college scholarship opportunities. As it was, he would miss his junior and senior high school years of academics, dating girls, going to dances, running track, earning Eagle Scout, and writing.

Earl had not picked the idea of gold mining casually. It was a preference that meshed with his pride and free spirit. But there was another, more pragmatic reason. During the Depression, the Portland shipyards would spray the inside of newly built ship's hulls with red lead, an emulsified substance that would preserve the bare steel hulls while they were idle during the economic downturn. Both Earl and Jack had done this work at the shipyard many nights for cash in a desperate effort to stay solvent and save their home and way of life.

Unfortunately, exposure to lead by working deep in the holds of ships had damaged their health. The red lead vapors were more toxic than first understood and it gave them both severe lead poisoning. This was a serious, potentially devasting illness that could lead to terrible headaches, seizures, and possibly death. When Earl first noticed his own early symptoms, he realized that Jack also suffered from the same symptoms—abdominal pain, loss of appetite, and fatigue.

Back in the thirties, medical science and treatments for lead poisoning were limited. One treatment was nutritional therapy, which suggested that milk was good for the liver and helped with detoxification. Also, soluble fiber such as found in pears, apples, and oatmeal were helpful. But the doctors' strongest suggestion was to spend a great deal of time working hard outside in the heat, which was thought to produce copious amounts of sweat to literally "get the lead out."

Rather than go to a distant hot place like Arizona, Earl chose to go gold mining along the Rogue River where summer temperatures would rise to 100°F or higher by 2:00 p.m. Jack and his dad camped out in the rugged, pristine Rogue River country at a place called Ennis Riffle, near Galice, named after Frank Ennis, a legendary miner who died in 1912. They worked the small creeks and the river for gold, lured there by newspaper reports of finding nuggets in the area. None of the reports talked about any kind of gold rush, just some significant discoveries and the dream of finding the "mother lode."

Earl was familiar with gold miners along the river. He had done some camping and fly-fishing for steelhead and cutthroat trout on the Rogue in better days before his money disappeared in the stock market crash and ship building came to a standstill.

The world had taken a couple of turns since the Gold Rush of the 1840s, however, and a lot of the obvious gold had been collected. The largest gold deposits that were left rested on bedrock many feet below the sand and gravel along the river. So gold mining for father-and-son Team Ingram involved digging down to that bedrock in search of the richest deposits. However, many factors like early spring flooding, erosion, decomposition, and disintegration of rock layer formations had shifted the gold supply around until, at times, it was there for the taking.

Jack and Earl did what was known as "placer mining." It meant they dug all day through the hard layers of river bottom toward the bedrock. They ran the gravel and sand muck material they had dug up through a sluice box, a wooden box sifter with steel ribs on the bottom, using the river and a water-wheel trough assembly they built as a source of continuous flushing power. Earl was right at home with his acumen for engineering and ingenuity for building an efficient water-delivery system out of old rusty pieces of steel scrap that miners had left along the river. It was the most exciting part of the day when they would find small flecks of gold and an occasional nugget laying in the bottom of the sluice box. They worked the sluice with bated breath!

Prospecting for gold appealed to Jack and his father's sense of pride as a worthier endeavor than the other choices available. And they felt they were successful at it. Even if their goal was not to get rich, at least they were making a living, earning enough to cover their daily needs. Along the Rogue, Earl and Jack, driven to survive, were adventurers at heart and imbued with the spirit of the original Forty-Niners. They definitely made their "claim" on the river!

Jack had good reason to be comfortable and competent camping on the river. He had earned merit badges in the Scouts that served him well during that time. He also had moral stamina and courage to go with "the program" as shown in his following original poem.

A CHALLENGE

If the game is full of scouting, Learning-doing exciting things;
If spirits bubble with living, Helping and giving brings;
Laughing turns to purpose, Skills to keen of mind;
A citizen is developing, Through scouting ways and kind;
There are no idle hands, Or minds that trouble brew;
This is the aim, crux and goal,
OF the BOY, SCOUTING and YOU.

Jack was a patient and proficient fisherman as well as a hunter with an interest in firearms and shooting competition. Father and son supplemented their store-bought food supplies by hunting for black-tailed deer, bear, quail, rabbit, and squirrel, which became their primary sustenance when conditions for fishing were poor.

Not only was Jack a good hunter, but when he bagged a deer or bear five miles or more from camp, he was perfectly adept at field-dressing the large game and bringing the meat back to camp. He also knew how to cook, smoke, salt, and store the meat and fish in a small four by four by eight foot log-cabin-like cottonwood smokehouse they built on a hill forty yards behind the camp.

On the Rogue, Jack spent countless hours on the riverbank basking in the summer sun when it got too hot to dig for "pay dirt"—gold. Not only did he enjoy it, it was part of the remedy and therapy to sweat out the lead poisoning in his system. After a day of hard shoveling in the sun, Jack saw that lead would actually blister to the surface of his skin through small pimples on his arms. Earl would often exclaim, "Thank God we're getting the lead out!"

The Rogue was a river of many moods. Further upstream its clear water, reflecting the deep, green forest along its edges, roared along with rapids and beautiful waterfalls marking its tumultuous run to the Pacific. From its birth high up at Crater Lake, it flowed sometimes easily, frequently with the fury of rapids and roaring white water, and then slowing to gentle currents where the gold was found.

The best gold deposits were found along the river as it passed through the Siskiyou Mountain rock formations. It was a picturesque site, with deer and bear foraging in rugged hillsides covered with ponderosa pine, Douglas fir, California black oak, alder, and cottonwood trees. Nearby, the aster meadows were filled with quail, deer, and rabbit, all dependent on the Rogue's fresh water as it continued its eternal journey to the sea.

Earl and Jack's home was a large canvas army staff tent that they supported with large poles cut from red alder and black cottonwood trees along the river. It was big enough for them and their supplies. Later, they built a twelve by sixteen-foot temporary log cabin with a tiny wood stove to stay warm in the winter.

Some nights the two slept out under the stars, with the splashing of river otters near the sand bar, the lonely wail of the loon, and haunting calls of two elusive Great Gray Owls as their lullaby. In the mornings, the cheerful chirping of songbirds and the cries of the ospreys and eagles provided their wake-up call.

Placer miners "Team Ingram" soon began to realize that unearthing gold was not like any other job. While payday is always a happy day on any job, finding "pay dirt" was another story! Payday for Team Ingram meant being thrilled at each discovery of gold found in the pay dirt after feeding their day's production of river sand and gravel material into their sluice along the river. Whether it was just flat gold fleck or a nugget, there was a certain amount of apprehension as well as anticipation and joy in discovering any gold. It gave them something to get up for in the morning and something to work for during the day.

They hid the largest and most valuable nuggets they found in the cavity of a ponderosa pine tree on a nearby hillside, and they placed the gold flecks in a glass vial for trading goods. Life was not safe in those desperate days along the river because murderous thieves would prey upon prospectors and steal their gold. Bringing the larger nuggets to the Galice assayer would invite thieves to focus on their claim and cache of gold in camp. Many gold miners were robbed and killed because they bragged about their finds and prosperity.

Every two months or so, Earl and Jack would drive back to Portland when the bottom of the Mason jar was covered with gold nuggets, anonymously cashing in their bounty to pay off old debts around town. They would always quickly drive back from Portland to Ennis Riffle, their camp and claim on the Rogue, because their claim could be subject to an opportunistic passerby. During these trips, Jack learned to drive the Model-A up and down Oregon's coastal highway.

Earl would take his glass vial of small gold flecks to the assayer's office, which was also a combination Galice Post Office and general store.

The flecks were considered "dirty gold" by the assayer for the purpose of not giving the miners the fair price. As a result, the assayer was reluctant to weigh the flecks at the full market value of "real" gold. So, with fairness in mind, Earl always kept one hand on his .38 Smith and Wesson pistol holstered on his waist and the other "on the scale," as the local old-timers tell the story today.

This practice of keeping the assayer/postmaster/storekeeper honest made Earl a legend on the Rogue, lending affirmation to his Texas farm days and Portland shipyard nickname of "Boss." Earl had grown up on a Texas farm before leaving home at fourteen and traveling the new rail to Denver, Colorado, and eventually adventuring over the mountains on horseback into the wilds of Oregon. He earned the nickname since he had proven to be "bossy" around his dad, Frank Ingram, and Frank's farm hands—cowboys.

In the troubled economic times of the Depression a man had to be careful, especially with all the homeless, desperate, penniless men trying to stay alive by roaming the Siskiyou Mountains and camps along the Rogue. The Rogue River country was a wilderness, and one's security was one's own personal responsibility. Anything could happen to a person along the Rogue!

But all in all, the Ingrams preferred it to the alternatives. Earl Ingram, as a Texan from the old West of the nineteenth century, knew how to handle a gun. Squeezing off a periodic .38 round or two near camp served as an explicit message to anyone that Camp Ingram was a claim on the river not to be challenged.

Earl taught Jack how to use guns, and they held target practice using their 1920 lever-action .300 Savage rifle around the general area of the ponderosa pine where they hid the Mason jar of gold nuggets—no one would ever sneak up on them from that direction! Earl was a dead-eye shot and Jack was close behind.

Other than during target practice, the area along the river where they were camped was as peaceful as church on Sunday. Jack would often swim in the river, which he was accustomed to doing in his birthday suit.

After bobbing about and floating on his back in the deep, cold-water river pools he would emerge, refreshed, and would fish for their dinner.

Steelhead fishing and Chinook salmon fishing at certain times of the year was not like fishing anywhere else. One did not even need a fishing rod in the early fall! Jack simply used a large, handmade rope net to capture the steady flow of spawning Chinook struggling to swim up the river near cold tributary streams to their birthplace.

One lure that Jack used was "pleasure bait." Jack would use colorful chewing gum on a small hook to lure salmon and cutthroat trout in the Rogue's tributary brooks and streams. Of course, he would chew all the sugar out of the gum first before sacrificing it to the fish. He had his best luck in the fall using this "sweet" technique. In the summer, Jack had little luck fly-fishing for steelhead salmon on the Rogue. He told his father about it. Earl said, "The trick is in the bait and in how you work your line. You've got to understand fly hatches on the river and bait like free salmon eggs during the characteristic spawning runs."

Jack's eyes said, "Tell me more."

Earl continued. "You use small pieces of red or orange cloth on a small hook to mimic salmon eggs for bait. Nothing else. Then you tie on a small piece of wood to act as a bobber, no weights."

Jack interrupted. "No weights. How do you get your bait down there?"

"That's just it. Steelhead don't hit on a bait sitting still on the end of a weighted line. You need to let the bait float around and bob in the river. It will move around like something live and the fish will hit it!"

"Can't wait to try that, though I'm not sure it will work."

"Try it!!"

Jack did try it and while Earl was in town getting supplies he landed two fat steelhead for dinner. He got busy cleaning them so they would be ready by the time his Dad got back from Galice. Dad was in town checking for mail and selling their last week's cache of gold flecks so he could pick up some camp supplies—milk, eggs, coffee, fruit, vegetables, back bacon, and beans to go with dinner.

Jack had finished cleaning the steelhead trout and had seasoned them with black pepper for the pan when he heard footsteps on the trail. Instinctively, he sprinted to the small cavity in the ponderosa pine where they hid their Mason jar and made sure it was hidden. His mind raced as he began formulating a plan to defend their camp while his father was away. Fortunately, the footsteps he had heard on the path was Earl, returning from town. Jack proudly showed off his catch and didn't mention his moment of anxiety.

The boy asked, "What's happening in town, Dad?"

"Nothing much, son, but there are some new faces and they have curious eyes. I kept a close watch all the way back."

"Any news from home?" Jack asked, his eyes on Earl's hand.

"Yes, I got a letter from my buddies at the Boilermaker's Union but there are no jobs in the shipyard or anywhere in Oregon, Washington, or California right now."

It was pretty much the same story every week on that score. But Earl always brought him back some treats, like milk which was not only essential for a growing boy, but more importantly it was part of the doctor's detoxification prescription for lead poisoning. And as for special treats that were not necessarily practical, he brought Jack's favorites—chocolates and chewing gum.

While Jack happily dug into his chocolate, Earl lapsed pensive for a while and then said, "Hard to believe a rich country like this could be going through such times."

"Yeah. I know," Jack said. He knew his father worried about the future. Jack had grown in many ways since the death of his mother, and he knew it was time to plot the path for his future.

Earl noticed the distant look in his son's blue eyes. "Still thinking about the navy?"

"Yeah, Dad, I am."

"You're right, gold digging isn't gonna get us rich and it's only temporary at best. Remember, son, regardless of what you do in life—work hard and always do the right thing."

"Beats trying to sell apples, or even worse, picking them."

Earl smiled. He then quietly said, "Let's face it, Jack, panning for gold is at least as hard as picking fruit. But out here we're . . . well, we're free. It's not much of a home, but we're on our own—self-sufficient. We've paid back all our debt and our reputation is intact. Being true to your word is one of the most important things in life."

During the Depression, many people in the world could not say the same. People walked away from debt, and never looked back.

Jack grinned. "You bet. Nothing better than being here." Jack raised his arm and pointed at the river. "Dad, home is where you make it, and it's here for us, on the river."

The next day, Earl and Jack decided to fly-fish from the large rocks in the middle of the river at Ennis with bamboo fly rods. Jack had his "lucky rock." Targeting a likely pool where the steelhead were rising, they cast flies as the sun began to rise into their box canyon. They moved to another spot near the red alders on the bank, and Jack cast his favorite fly, improving his technique, until he got a terrific strike. The steelhead was at least five pounds. Jack was quickly learning the art of fly-fishing—no lost leaders and no lost flies—and he was spending another perfect day with Dad on the river.

More importantly, Earl thought it was good to take the day off from digging to fly-fish with his son!

As they sat by the fire sipping the last dregs of their coffee, admiring their catch, and watching the river roll by in the deepening twilight, Jack realized it had been another a magical time on the river. The day cooled, and the sun turned crimson, silhouetting the towering cottonwoods and firs on the bank. For Jack, becoming an expert fly-fisherman like his dad, and camping out with him in Rogue River country, under the towering Siskiyou Mountains, was the best of all worlds. And yet, he was beginning to think of distant lands and the many things he wanted to accomplish.

Young Jack made several interesting acquaintances during his stay on the River. To his great surprise, he met his idol, Zane Grey, who had a cabin further down the river. Zane loved to fish large spans of the river, one of which happened to be Ennis Riffle—the Ingram claim. For any red-blooded American boy growing up back then, Zane Grey was an icon; he was legendary, and his stories were breathtaking. His tales of the old West and of adventure naturally stirred a boy's imagination. Any boy who liked to read would find himself immersed in Zane Grey's best-selling books and articles.

Grey was an avid fisherman and Jack enjoyed reading his articles about fishing. So, when he actually met and fished with the famous author, he was thrilled beyond belief. It seemed that his old English teacher's comment that he wrote like the famous Zane Grey had come full circle, at least in potential. Earl, Jack, Zane, and Zane's nice women friends spent an entire afternoon fly-fishing together from Ennis to Galice, raising steelhead with simple, colorful flies. Of course, Jack knew all the best holes to fish, and Zane seemed very happy. Zane told Jack and Earl many stories about his trips and travels that day and into the evening hours. Feasting on steelhead, Jack listened, understanding the significance in all that was happening.

Jack also befriended an old Spanish-American War veteran named Crowe. Jack spent many hours helping Crowe split wood at his cabin while listening to his stories about the "splendid little war," as it was called in those days, and learning a lot of life lessons that he otherwise may not have understood. Topics spanned war, guns, how to sharpen tools—especially shovels and axes—hunting, curing meat, gold panning tips, Indian lore, and the importance of staying away from the wild women who made their living on the mountain near Galice.

In a way, Crowe's stories enhanced Jack's image of and boyish yearning for adventure, and Jack's thoughts often returned to a future in the navy. Old Crowe told him, "The army and Teddy Roosevelt's Rough Riders covered themselves in glory at San Juan Hill outside of Santiago. But the navy won two glorious and famous battles, one at Manila Bay in the Philippines where they wiped out the Spanish fleet with no casualties, other than exhausted, overheated men shoveling coal into the ships' boilers during the battle, and again outside of Santiago Harbor in Cuba

Ennis Riffle - Ingram Rogue River Gold Claim

where they defeated the Spanish Navy with only one casualty. Admiral Dewey's victory at Manila made him a national naval hero. There were honors and grand ticker-tape parades in New York City."

The high-pitched squeal of the train's brakes startled Jack as the train slowed to pull into the next station. Jack's daydreams of what he had experienced on the Rogue River made him think about the skills he had acquired and life lessons that he learned. He knew that those adventures and experiences would benefit him as he faced his next chapter in the military.

He'd gained an appreciation of the essential elements of life, benefiting from hard work, friendships, and some of life's best natural gifts—fresh water, natural food, private shelter, and other riches from the land. He didn't realize it at the time but overcoming life's adversities——losing his mother and his home and not having a consistent job—had given him a sense of independence and personal worth.

Jack's first great leadership character trait was his *self-worth*!

Chapter Two
Bluejacket

Jack arrived at the U.S. Naval Recruit Training Center in San Diego after a long trip down the Oregon and California coast. Like any new recruit, he was filled with anxiety, mostly about the unexpected. He had heard tales of the rigors of boot camp and he was hoping a lot of it was exaggerated; still, he was geared up and in great shape from his two-year stint on the Rogue. Armed with a small, still-empty pocket journal called "Trips and Travels" that his dad had given him, he was ready to fill it with navy stories!

The navy boot camp occupied a low stretch of tideland beside San Diego Bay. Jack's stint at boot camp was to be three months before being assigned to sea duty. It was April 25, 1935, and the young man, now eighteen years old, was ready in many ways for military indoctrination, and it did not take him long to get into the full swing of things.

He was prepared physically and mentally for the rigorous training. What he was not ready for was the navy's obsession with cleanliness! While in training Jack found himself scrubbing everything from his own clothes to the barracks floor, the company yard, and the latrines.

Fortunately, Jack found some of the other aspects of boot camp more appealing. Basic training included: firing range target practice with the .08 Springfield rifle, the obstacle course, swim tests, survival training, abandon ship drill, seamanship training on long boats, knot tying, and much more. Jack was a standout!

On June 6 an article in Portland's *Oregonian* newspaper highlighted Jack as an "Oregon Boy" winning "Weekly Honor Man of his company at the United States Naval Training Station in San Diego for the week ending May 31." The article went on to say, "The honor is bestowed upon the recruit who is outstanding in personal appearance, in attention to duty, and in his ability to profit from instruction."

Upon arrival in San Diego, Jack was more prepared than others for the military culture and its purpose. The goal was to take all the *civilian* out of the recruits and recast and reform them into durable seamen in the United States Navy. Jack's new bible was the seventh edition of *Bluejacket's Manual*, a nine-hundred-plus-page catechism that prepared recruits for life as sailors. By the time Jack left recruit training on July 27 he felt like he was already "salty," a term used to suggest how seasoned you were as a sailor.

In later years, like many sailors, Jack would remember the great transition he underwent in boot camp. From the first night in the barracks listening to the occasional sobbing around the big room from kids not so prepared, to the joy on graduation day when the new sailors felt invigorated, Jack recognized that it had been quite a journey. Now the sailors were buoyed by the experience and, as healthy, fit young men, they prepared themselves for their boyish dreams of adventure in the navy that had stirred their imaginations for so long.

Jack was very proud of his first assignment, the battleship USS *Pennsylvania*. The *Pennsylvania BB-38* was the lead ship of the Pennsylvania class of United States Navy super-dreadnought battleships. She was the flagship of the Pacific fleet, sister ship of USS *Arizona*, and one of the largest vessels in the navy, carrying 1,358 men. In fact, the battleship was considered the backbone of the navy until the "Pacific War" (the Pacific theater of World War II) brought on a new naval doctrine, one that proved that the aircraft carrier was the future and was to become the most important ship in the navy.

Jack couldn't wait to get to Seattle to get started.

He was transferred from San Diego to Seattle aboard an oil tanker, USS *Kanawha*, which provided the recruit with a vivid and graphic comparison of the two vessels. The oil tanker was a ship that reeked of smelly fuel oil, and it provided an uncomfortable ride to USS *Pennsylvania*—a sleek battlewagon, which at the time was the pride of the navy.

Jack knew that he could have been assigned to a much less glamorous naval craft like a supply ship or an oil tanker. A battleship was the

Battleship *Pennsylvania BB-38*

Jack - Top-side on the *Pennsylvania*

pride of the navy, queen of the fleet, and a plum assignment, especially for a new recruit. The young seaman loved his first ship and "family" photos of his happy face while aboard her proved it.

His job aboard the *Pennsylvania* was pointer on the starboard five-inch broadside battery. There were twenty-two five-inch gun mounts on USS *Pennsylvania.* The gun fired fifty-four-pound projectiles and a case assembly, which included a fifteen-pound powder charge. The projectiles were used for anti-aircraft, fixed target, sky illuminators, and smoke. The ballistic performance obtained could reach 2,600 feet per second: horizontal range of 54,000 feet and vertical range of 37,300 feet. Jack's crew's sustained firing rate was eighteen rounds per minute!

The pointer, in a gun crew of twenty-five men, was one of the more skilled jobs. Whereas the more routine jobs in the gun turret involved handling gun powder and ammunition and loading the projectiles, the pointer was a job requiring aptitude. The pointer controls the mount elevation and firing. He sits in the left-hand corner with his optical sight, hand wheels, and elevation drive in front of him. On his right about elbow high is a box called the elevation indicator regulator.

Sailors swabbing the deck

When the pointer sees the target in his crosshairs he controls the gun's elevation with his hand wheels. At the command of the Mount Captain he fires the gun electrically by squeezing the firing key. So Jack went from squeezing off .30 caliber (one-third-inch-diameter) bullets on the Rogue to firing five-inch-diameter shells full of anti-aircraft ordnance, like a large shotgun, on USS *Pennsylvania*. Jack was in his glory! There were many routine practice sessions learning and perfecting this job for the whole gun turret crew.

Jack's life aboard the *Pennsylvania* as a seaman first class was routine:

5:30 a.m. Reveille (wake-up call) by a bugle over a loudspeaker. Reveille was followed immediately by morning hygiene and housekeeping, making up bunks, airing bedding, and cleaning up quarters.

7:30 a.m. Assembly. This is a formation in which every man falls in to his assigned place in the formation where he is addressed by his superiors, petty officers, or officers. At this formation, a man could report for sick call or special assignments.

8:00 a.m. Breakfast. Breakfast consisted of some combination of cereal, eggs, bacon, sausage, pancakes, French toast, coffee, juice, and milk—always milk. Jack related that he had more for breakfast in the navy than he ate all day on the Rogue.

9:00 a.m. Report for assignments and tasks. A sailor could be assigned one or more task such as maintenance, holystoning (see below) and swabbing the decks, or scraping, painting, and cleaning any facet of the ship. Jack certainly knew all about red lead and the precautions in its use.

Noon. Lunch. Lunch typically consisted of sandwiches, vegetables, fruit, and, as always, milk—Jack's favorite beverage. One lunch and dinner dish became a longtime navy quip of Jack's—chipped beef on toast, or what he disgustingly called "foreskins on a raft"—not his favorite!

1:00 p.m. Back to work.

4:30 p.m. Workday finished. Released from duty.

5:30 p.m. Dinner. Dinner was a hearty meal that usually consisted of chicken, turkey, pork, or beef dishes with plenty of mashed potatoes and vegetables. Jack's favorite dessert was ice cream.

After dinner was free time and, if Jack was not on watch or some special duty, he was free to do as he wished. He often used the time to take care of personal chores, or he would spend the time reading, studying, letter writing, telling stories about the Rogue River, or listening to others' stories from around the country and world. Often Jack got involved in various games such as cards, chess, checkers, or backgammon. There were even movie nights, when he watched the latest news reels.

At any time of day and night, battle station drills were routinely called and everyone practiced manning their battle stations. There were also other drills such as fire drill, abandon ship drill, and so on. The crew was judged on the time it took them to get to their stations and their efficiency at their battle stations. Of course, most of this was practice, but Jack took pride in being safe, fast, efficient, and effective.

A routine job for the lowest ranks was holystoning the deck, sometimes done before swabbing, or mopping, the deck. This involved the use of a holystone, a large, rectangular sandstone block with a hole in the middle in which a peg was inserted. The sailors would get on their knees and, shoulder to shoulder from bow to stern, push and pull the stone back and forth along the white-oak wooden deck, which had been sprayed down with salt water. It was said that anybody who spent that much time on his knees had to be holy and praying; thus, the term holystoning.

Sailors had to be up on deck three hours before light to accomplish this task on the *Pennsylvania*. Holystoning success meant that all the dirt, grease, and grime would be cleaned off the oak planking resulting in a glistening white deck by sunrise. The sailors, exhausted and sore from the task, would say, "Thank God the old man (captain) is happy!"

Another routine job for the lowest ranks was galley duty. This was basically washing dishes, pots, and pans, peeling potatoes, setting up tables, serving meals, or doing any other job the ship's cooks would assign. Finally, after all meals, the galley had to be cleaned according to regulations. Men assigned to galley duty had to be up two hours before reveille to get ready to serve breakfast. They would be on duty until after dinner and everything was cleaned to the cook's satisfaction by around eight in the evening. Fortunately, Jack only had galley duty once.

Jack would rather holystone the deck every morning than be called for galley duty. Years later Jack, who never swore when angered, could frequently be heard to use the phrase, "Son of a Sea Cook," which resonated from his one bad experience with a cook on galley duty.

Another duty was starboard or port watch duty in which the sailor was required to stand aerial and sea lookout or simply stand guard in an area. The shifts were four hours on and four hours off. Where you were assigned on the ship would determine your watch duty. If you were on the flying squad you would look for and report any flooding or smoke.

If you were on the quartermaster watch you were on the bridge, either at the helm steering the ship or recording every order the officer of the deck (OD) gave. In the engine room, you were looking for any sign of trouble such as oil or water leaks.

Jack sometimes had watch duty in which he was required to ring the ship's bell. The ship's bell was used to indicate time aboard the ship and to regulate the timing of the duty watches. There were eight bell tolls, one each half-hour of a four-hour watch.

Today, USS *Pennsylvania*'s actual bell that Jack rang in 1936 is located at the Wagner Building, home of the ROTC program on the Pennsylvania State University campus. It serves as a reminder of Jack's service as a young sailor.

Each watch had specific duties and eventually a man got to learn all the duties he might be called on to perform during his watch. One of Jack's favorite duties was being the runner for the officer of the deck. This duty entailed running messages to and from others on the ship. Jack was known as a very fast runner. He was also personable in his delivery, enticing officers of the deck to favor him for the task. He always took the time to ask good questions and listen to their thoughts and advice.

In December, while aboard the *Pennsylvania*, Jack participated in seasonal fleet gunnery drills called "problems" in the Pacific. His primary duty in those early months was being a gunner. He would drill with his shipmates by day and enjoy shore leave with them some nights, building camaraderie and lifelong friendships.

Before any shore leave, the "Pennsy" would issue "dummy bags" for the sailors' personal protection. A dummy bag was a small canvas sandbag that was tied to a sailor's forearm with a cotton string hidden under their uniform. With a quick downward thrust of an arm, a sailor could quickly have the sandbag come to rest in his fist, ready to pack a powerful punch for personal protection. And in those days, there were many thugs and desperate thieves who tried to take advantage of sailors on leave and mug them late at night.

Camaraderie was strong aboard the *Pennsylvania*, and Jack made some good friends while serving on the ship. One of his favorite extracurricular activities with some of his buddies was boxing. Back then, boxing was among the most popular sports in America. On Saturday nights, many men, both civilian and military, were glued to their radios for the Saturday night fights. There were many boxing heroes at the time, and men considered boxing the manliest of sports. Jack and his buddies were no exception.

There was no formal boxing program on the *Pennsylvania*, but the hotly contested matches, known as "smokers," were held on the fantail on select Friday nights. Sailors who participated in these events were given certain extra privileges such as time off from duty to train and prepare for their Friday night bouts. Jack, nicknamed "Ingy," became very good at it, earning a record of 13 and 0—until he got his nose broken, which ended his short boxing career.

Jack's two chief petty officer aerologist friends supported his boxing, betting and winning a lot of money on him. Their friendship got him interested in their specialty, aerography, the preferred name in the navy for weather reporting.

Jack learned all that he could about aerography. Because he was a highly skilled typist, he volunteered to help his friends by typing weather reports late at night. These neatly typed reports earned the aerologists kudos from the skipper, so the aerologists were inclined to help Jack, giving him several special considerations.

He would get the best food—steak and potatoes and plenty of ice cream. In addition, he had extra time off from duty and the special privilege of sleeping on the floor of the much-cooler upper deck of the ship rather than the hot, stuffy, smelly berthing quarters five-hammock-racks deep.

Back in those days, typed weather reports were not common, and Jack gave his friends the idea to give the captain a typed report every day. They took credit, and Jack was happy. Rarely did Jack outwardly seek recognition. He was more interested in the team benefitting from his work. He always had faith in people that credit would be given where credit was due.

Jack's recognized worth for producing real-time, intelligent, typewritten and oral briefs would come years later. Jack's ability to type clear, concise weather reports became his hallmark. The captain liked to have a written report or brief to refer to rather than making a quick decision about operations from an oral weather report, relying on memory.

Jack's early journal entries show a glimpse of his sea duty for the rest of 1935 and 1936. On December 17, he sailed into San Pedro, California, where he transferred to communication duty. The *Pennsylvania* then left for the navy yard, and Jack was temporarily assigned to three months duty on the battleship USS *New Mexico.*

Jack felt fortunate for having been assigned to the *Pennsylvania* and, with a new sailor's love of his ship, he made the best of the temporary change in assignment while the Pennsy was in the yard being fitted with new equipment.

On April 12, 1936, Jack was back on the Pennsy sailing for Balboa, Canal Zone (C.Z.), Panama, and arrived at 0700 on the 9th of May. This foreign destination and the upcoming cruise to Asia was what the young sailor craved and was one of the many reasons he had signed up. He was happy to get this cruise because so many of his classmates from boot camp were assigned to supply ships and smaller war ships.

On May 18, 1936, the *Pennsylvania,* with Jack back aboard, left Balboa, C.Z. and sailed for the equator. For a young sailor, this was the height of adventure. Sailing at latitudes 00.00 n 81.00 w, the ship crossed the equator at 0830. This initiated a shellback ceremony before the ship returned to Panama.

A time-honored tradition, the Order of Neptune Ritual dates back four hundred years of Western seafaring. The ceremony marks the transformation from a "slimy pollywog," a sailor who has not yet crossed the equator, to a seasoned "shellback." Another name for a shellback is a son or daughter of Neptune, hence the name of the ritual. In lore, it was a test of a sailor's seaworthiness, but in reality it was simply a tradition that the men liked because it involved a lot of fun and camaraderie.

When a ship crosses the equator, King Neptune appears on board to judge charges brought against pollywogs. The charge is that they

Pennsylvania Shellback Plank – May 20, 1936

are only posing as sailors. Senior crew members, often those who have been shellbacks the longest, participate in the ceremony by dressing up in costumes and playing roles in King Neptune's court. Often, the ship's captain played the role of King Neptune himself. The pollywogs must then pay homage to the god of the sea.

The ceremony is a day of festival involving good food and drink as well as a welcome relief from the daily shipboard routine and chores. There is a lot of hilarity and "monkeyshines" (pranks) and it is all done in the spirit of good fun. But its main purpose was to build and strengthen camaraderie among the seafaring crew and, over the years, various naval services and seafarers have devised their own versions of this ritual.

Having survived his Order of Neptune initiation, Jack Ingram had become an official shellback, so he was feeling salty like an experienced sailor, proud to be on the *Pennsylvania.*

On Monday, May 25, the *Pennsylvania* left Balboa, C.Z., and sailed for San Pedro, California, arriving at 1000 hours on Saturday. On July 6, Jack transferred from communications to duty as aerography striker. His chief petty officer friends brought Jack to the attention of the captain and he was acknowledged for his report writing/brief expertise. He was now recognized as the silent author behind the typing of briefs (weather reports), and he began running them directly to the captain for daily operations.

The ship sailed for Honolulu, Hawaii, on July 7, 1936, at 1400 hours. And on July 17, Jack was rated seaman second class. Jack's weather report duty elevated his stature in the navy hierarchy. It separated him from swabbys, or deck sailors. He now had an important job with new responsibilities and, on the 16th of August, Jack was elevated to seaman first class. Here again, as a conscientious young man and a regular navy sailor, Jack appreciated every promotion, and seaman first class was the beginning of the climb up the long ladder of the navy.

Jack sailed back to Long Beach on the *Pennsylvania* and arrived on Saturday the 22nd of August at 0800 hours. By the fall of that year, on the 9th of October, Jack took his first seven-day leave. He, of course, went home to Portland, Oregon, for leave. As a young navy man, Jack enjoyed returning home to see his family and friends around town.

Back aboard the Pennsy, he sailed for Hunters Point, San Francisco, arriving on the 9th of November. On the 12th, the fleet fired a nineteen-gun salute for the opening ceremony of the San Francisco–Oakland Bay Bridge. Jack loved the pomp and pageantry of such naval exercises and he enjoyed his participation, shoulder-to-shoulder "at ease" with his shipmates encircling the entire circumference of the ship in their dress-blue wool uniforms.

In December of 1936, Jack noted in his journal that he purchased U.S. savings bonds (maturity value $25.00 each), an indication of his thrift, even as a young man. Many young sailors would blow their entire pay on leave at exotic ports of call, while young Jack was mature enough to realize the benefits of saving.

The end of 1936 marked the end of Jack's introduction to sea duty. Next would be an exciting new phase of his naval career. He received word that his request was granted by the Bureau of Naval Personnel (BUPERS), and he'd be headed to aerographer's school in Lakehurst, New Jersey, for a five-month course of instruction at the U.S. Naval Air Station. His two aerology chief petty officer friends on board the *Pennsylvania* kept their promise to recommend young Jack to the navy's premier weather school because he had made them look good by typing in-depth, factual, and colorful reports for months.

Jack was excited by his acceptance into this prestigious navy training course. It would be his first professional step up in the navy. He was determined to do well, and he studied hard. The training was crucial to him, and he took it quite seriously.

In 1937, there were only seventy-five aerologists in the U.S. military who forecasted the weather. Weather training was relatively new in the navy, and it was furthered by the development and expansion of aircraft carrier operations.

Some of Jack's friends somehow thought that he was going to study aerial photography. This confusion came from the misunderstanding of the term aerography (study of weather). But, of course, the study of weather included study of atmospheric patterns, map work, high-level math, meteorology, ocean dynamics, storm patterns, and everything else that was then known about weather.

The two chief petty officers had initially bet on Jack, the boxer, to make money for themselves. They let him sleep above decks and fed him well to protect their investment, only to realize that Jack had a lot more to offer when he volunteered to anonymously type their daily weather reports for the captain. Jack was mature for his age, and he had learned to always work hard to make others look good. In a very humble manner, he took care of others before himself—highlighting the strengths of his shipmates and complementing their talents to accomplish a task.

Discipline, focus, and personal goal-setting were central to Jack's early years in the navy. Jack's respect for his mentors' advice and his ability to develop friendships positioned him for future growth and advancement.

Jack had started his career with a love of adventure and travel, which would later turn into a serious navy career where people would come to depend on him, as a humble warrior, for advice and advancement. Jack never wanted anything in return because he wanted to help others in any way possible.

Jack's second great leadership character trait was *humility*!

Chapter Three

Hindenburg Class

Sailors, as seagoing men, have always had an abiding interest in the weather, from John Paul Jones, a hero of the American Revolution, to Admiral "Bull" Halsey, of WWII fame. Jones had a barometer aboard his ship *Bonhomme Richard* which gave him some chance of foretelling an approaching storm. Halsey had much more technology and was surrounded by meteorological expertise.

With the advent of a fleet air arm, both fixed-wing (heavier-than-air) and dirigible (lighter-than-air), weather forecasting had become even more important. The U.S. Navy has, as does any seagoing organization, a vital interest in weather and predicting weather for the safety and operational ability of its ships and aircraft. As a practical matter, an accurate weather forecast is decidedly one of the most important pieces of tactical information when preparing a navy strike force for battle. Many a mission has been planned and the battle won or lost depending upon weather conditions and the commander's ability to accurately forecast operations. For example, in the sixteenth century, storms scattered the Spanish Armada so badly they were isolated and cut to pieces by the British.

Young Jack was excited with his new assignment to study aerology at the Lakehurst Naval Air Station. His friends and shipmates from the *Pennsylvania* were true to their promise and helped him prepare for the school by tutoring and coaching him. Most helpful were the months of daily typed weather briefings he prepared for the captain of the *Pennsylvania.*

After traveling by train across the country to the East Coast, his first such trip east, he came to appreciate his country and all its beauty. He made a special mental note of how much the mountains and streams in central Pennsylvania from Altoona to the Susquehanna River in Harrisburg reminded him of southern Oregon.

Jack started aerology school in late January of 1937. He would study physics, math, meteorology, and, though it seemed mundane, typing. Often, he would type and edit reports for his classmates. They in turn would help him with subjects like math. Because of the Depression and the need to go to work with his father for a living, Jack had to leave high school. Without the advantage of an entire high school education, his friends' help and tutoring became even more valuable to him.

When he graduated as an enlisted man, he would be qualified to identify surface and upper air observations, elements of dynamic meteorology, and would understand the basics of weather forecasting at sea, on land, and in the air . . . especially in the air.

A journal entry dated February 10, 1937, reports "Two weeks of school. Plenty of work. Passed entrance exams. One third through school." Jack undertaking this course was a testament to his innate intelligence considering that this was a scientific, math-based course taken by a student with a tenth-grade education. And he was still quite young. On March 15, 1937, the young sailor celebrated his twentieth birthday.

In April Jack bought a Plymouth Deluxe Coupe. The car was dark blue, drove well, and had been driven two hundred miles. As with every young man, his first car was a treasure and a source of pride. Jack had taken the choice of car very seriously, and he put a great deal of thought into the decision. He surveyed his entire class and other buddies on the base to ask them what car they would buy if they had the resources—the Plymouth Deluxe was the winner!

As May of 1937 approached, and Jack continued school, across the sea in Germany a giant airship called the *Hindenburg* was preparing to depart on a trip to New York where it would moor at the Lakehurst Naval Air Station in New Jersey. Lakehurst was one of the naval air stations that was equipped to handle dirigibles. Naval Air Station Commander C.E. Rosendahl had planned that Jack's class would get a tour of the ship once it was moored at the base. Everyone on base knew that the *Hindenburg* would arrive on May 6, 1937, at 1700 hours, and excitement grew.

Aerography Class, 1937 (Hindenburg Class) . Jack in top row, third from left.

The *Hindenburg* was a marvel for its time and was the pride of the Nazi propaganda machine which touted (in subtle terms) the superiority of German technology. Whereas it took an ocean liner over a week to cross the Atlantic, the *Hindenburg*, the largest airship ever built at eight-hundred-feet long, did it in two days with as much luxury (or more) as any cruise liner like the Queen Mary.

Due to political and economic reasons, the airship used hydrogen (a flammable gas) instead of helium. The only natural helium reserves in the world were in Texas, and the United States did not want to give the Germans any helium. Moreover, it was not practical to ship the helium to Germany in those days; it was too costly.

Since the weather was rainy and less than favorable as the German airship approached Lakehurst, the commanding officer (CO) of the base advised the *Hindenburg* to delay its mooring. So the captain of the *Hindenburg* turned around and made a slow pass over New York City, giving the passengers a spectacular view. Then the ship cruised south as far as Asbury Park, New Jersey, and then over toward Lakehurst. All this time, Jack and his aerography class/landing crew stood out in the rain waiting for their opportunity to moor the airship to a huge mast. Finally, Commander Rosendahl radioed that conditions had improved and it was favorable to land the airship.

Jack was part of the group which was to catch the mooring lines tossed down to help the ship dock its nose to the mooring mast. It was a plum assignment and the sailors on the mooring party were excited at the prospect of handling the famous airship.

As the great airship slowly maneuvered into position, its rear engines nudging it closer to the mooring mast, Jack and his mates watched the *Hindenburg* in awe. It was their first experience with an airship and they were speechless. They stood on the huge landing field looking up at the enormity of its size. Jack and the other men started to reach for and grab the mooring lines of the huge ship, attempting to steady her into position. It seemed kind of fun as they worked together, all buoyed by the excitement and celebrity of the massive dirigible.

As they worked, the radio announcer Herbert Morrison was reporting, "It's practically standing still now. They have dropped the ropes from the nose. Our sailors on the ground have grabbed them. It's starting to rain again." Seconds later he reported, "It's slackening off. Now the rear motors are keeping the ship steady."

Suddenly, his voice raised in full panic, he blurted, "It has burst into flames! It's on fire! It's crashing! Oh my, get out of the way, please! It has burst into flames. This is the worst calamity in the world! There's smoke! There's fire! Oh, the humanity! All the passengers are screaming around here."

Within thirty-seven seconds, the German icon, the largest airship ever built, was on the ground, its skeletal steel frame standing out in stark reality as the canvas of the dirigible burned fiercely.

Jack helped tend to the aftermath of the disaster. Thirty-six people were killed, and many were injured. It was a chaotic scene on the ground as the navy landing party attempted to deal with the fire as well as to pull people out of the burning wreckage, all while trying to stay safe themselves. In the distance, the wail of sirens played counterpoint to the noisy chaos that broke the once cool, wet, quiet afternoon.

After the *Hindenburg* hit the ground, Jack and his classmates ran back into the flames to save people, time and time again, until no one was left to be found alive. They saved at least fifteen people from perishing that day. It was the end of the *Hindenburg* and the end of an era!

In an article about Jack's role in the disaster, *The Oregonian* quoted Jack as saying, "I had never seen the ship and I was waiting for months for it to arrive. I was really expecting to see some spectacular sight—I did all right!"

Jack went on to say, "My part of the ground crew was directly beneath the ship waiting to grab the control booth rope when it came down. We were watching the ship when, Holy Pete, the whole bow was on fire. I didn't know what to do. It was like a horrible nightmare. I just stood there with my mouth open until my buddy socked me on the arm and said, 'Run!' We really made tracks then and the faster we ran the hotter it got. The heat was so intense that the next morning some of the girders were molten, twisted, pretzels of steel."

"After that thing went off we didn't expect to see a living soul come out. You know when three fourths of a person's body is burned he is supposed to die, but so many of those people were so badly burned they looked like mummies. And they're still alive to tell about it. It was a ghastly scene, a macabre spectacle, straight out of your worst nightmare!"

The *Oregonian* account continued, "Ingram said that had the explosion occurred after the ship was moored, not only would the ground

Four Images of *Hindenburg* disaster (Jack's personal photos from a photographer)

crew and spectators have been caught but Lakehurst itself 'blown off the map.' The reason being that since Lakehurst was a naval air station that handled the *Hindenburg*, large supplies of hydrogen are stored in tanks at the field, it undoubtedly would have been ignited."

To give an idea of the intensity of the heat from the fire, Jack and his mates had been wearing their thick wool peacoats during a day of constant cold rain. As a result, by the time the big airship had arrived and landing operations began, their peacoats were soaked through until they were getting heavy with water. Jack said, "Right after the disaster, our peacoats were completely dried out!" "We were really pretty lucky," Jack said. "But I hope I never see anything like it again. None of us could sleep for a couple of nights afterwards."

Jack made no attempt to conceal his contempt for the "ghouls" who, after seeing the catastrophe, had to be forcibly beaten off to prevent them from obtaining grisly souvenirs of the disaster. Jack's CO gave the order for Jack and his classmates, sailors and marines, to surround the skeleton of the ship and guard it all night. Several opportunistic scavengers were physically stopped from collecting anything from the airship. A few of these ghouls were carted away in ambulances from a good old navy boxer's left-and-right combination or two, never to be seen on the base again and no longer clinging to *Hindenburg* tea cups or passenger jewelry they tried to steal.

Later Jack wrote in his journal: "It is all over now. It has been almost a month since the ill-fated *Hindenburg* exploded with the loss of 36 lives. Hope to God I never again see such a spectacle and I thank God for my life." Another entry read: "Received commendation from CO for performance of duty during loss of *Hindenburg*."

The *Oregonian* newspaper account relayed further, "The former Commerce High student was one of 26 picked men attending the navy's aerology school at Lakehurst. Since enlisting here in 1935 he has been on the U.S.S. *Pennsylvania* and will shortly rejoin the Pacific fleet at San Diego. Portland friends might have some difficulty recognizing him as he has grown three inches and added 35 pounds during his two years with the fleet."

NA4/P15 U. S. NAVAL AIR STATION (Cy)
LAKEHURST, N.J.

30 June 1937

From: The Commanding Officer.

To : **INGRAM, Jack Richard, Sealc, #393-17-14, U.S. Navy.**

Via : **Commanding Officer, Receiving Ship, San Diego, Calif.**

SUBJECT: Commendation for performance of duty on occasion of loss of Airship HINDENBURG.

1. During and following the destruction of the airship HINDENBURG by fire at this station on the afternoon of 6 May 1937, the conduct and performance of duty of the personnel attached to this station were of such high order as to have evoked the most favorable and wide spread comment and praise. Every officer and every enlisted man attached to and then on duty in this command was on this trying occasion called upon for a maximum of effort, efficiency and resourcefulness, in most cases beyond the ordinary call of duty, whether serving in the ground crew or at any other of the varied and difficult tasks that arose as a result of the disaster. The Commanding Officer considers that in every case such duties were performed in an outstanding manner reflecting credit upon the Naval Service; this was so consistently true as to render it impracticable to single out individuals for special recognition.

2. The Commanding Officer therefore commends you for your efficient, resourceful and highly creditable performance of duty on the subject occasion.

C E Rosendahl

C. E. Rosendahl.

Commendation from Rosendahl

The Nazis were humiliated. This happened before the war started, when the Nazi party was ascending due to its powerful propaganda machine. For a long time they had touted the *Hindenburg* as an example of superior German craftsmanship. But after this disaster it was rumored that a design flaw had been what brought the airship to its tragic end.

Other dispatches and accounts include:

"Harrisburg, Pennsylvania May 7, 1937

"To Secretary of the navy, Washington, D.C.

"Major Camille Vinet, Instructor of Aeronautics for Commonwealth of Pennsylvania eye witness to the explosion and resultant destruction of Hindenburg has just reported to me. His strongest impression was the magnificent heroism of Commander Rosendahl (Commander of the Lakehurst Naval Air Station) and his men of the U.S. Navy who dove into the inferno again and again utterly 'regardless of their safety,' whose bravery and heroic actions alone saved at least fifteen lives.

"Signed George H. Earle, Governor of Pennsylvania"

Another message received at Lakehurst read:

"Berlin 7 May 1937

"Commander Rosendahl, Lakehurst, USA

"For the heroic rescue of the survivors of the German airship Hindenburg when she was destroyed at her landing at the airship port Lakehurst, I express to you and your brave men my warmest thanks and appreciation. This unreserved help of the American airmen in coming to the rescue of their German comrades is beautiful proof of the spirit which links the airmen of all nations.

"Signed German Ministry of Aviation, Colonel-General Göring"

Followed by the message sent to Germany:

"Lakehurst 8 May 1937

"Minister of Aviation Colonel-General Göring, Berlin

"American airship personnel deeply appreciate your generous message and extend sincere sympathy to Germany and those families bereaved through Hindenburg loss. Stop. We are thankful circumstance

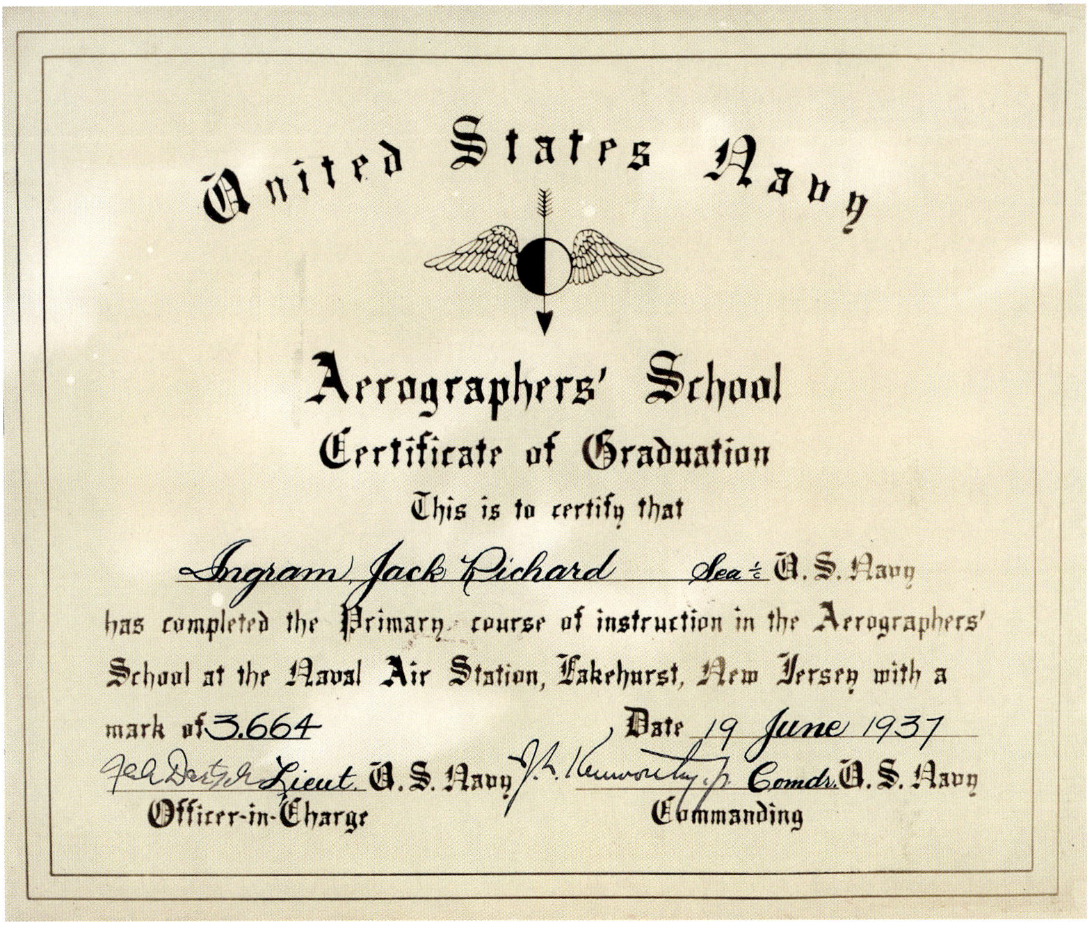
United States Navy

Aerographers' School

Certificate of Graduation

This is to certify that

Ingram, Jack Richard Sea 1/c U. S. Navy

has completed the Primary course of instruction in the Aerographers' School at the Naval Air Station, Lakehurst, New Jersey with a mark of 3.664 Date 19 June 1937

Lieut. U. S. Navy Comdr. U. S. Navy

Officer-in-Charge Commanding

Aerographers' School Certificate

permitted us to serve our German airship comrades in their distress. Stop. We applaud and admire your announced determination to continue airship progress.

"Signed Commander Rosendahl"

Message received from Germany:

"Frankfurt on Main 9 May 1937

"Commander Rosendahl Naval Station Lakehurst

"For personal assistance and for sacrifices made at time of destruction of airship Hindenburg and for personal warm interest and care of our comrades, to you and your assistant in Lakehurst, our sincere and deep felt gratitude also to the family of the ground crew member who was killed, our heartfelt sympathy, Long live airships!"

"Signed Deutsche Zeppelin Reederei

"(German Airship Transport Company)"

In June, Jack graduated third in his class of twenty-six, and he was a navy aerographer. Even though his class was designated in 1937 as "A Class" at the navy's aerology school, his class would be forever known as the "Hindenburg Class" for their heroism and bravery running back to the burning airship, saving lives that fateful day in May, and standing watch all night to protect the scene of the lost passengers and crew. Jack had experienced one of the worst catastrophic events in U.S. history. He revealed his selfless bravery by running back to the *Hindenburg* to rescue, console, and administer first aid emergency treatment to passengers who suffered horrific burns.

Jack's third great leadership character trait was *bravery*!

Chapter Four
Time to Be an Aerographer

Jack was rising in the navy. Having been a "swabby," whose duties included only manual labor like holystoning and swabbing decks, manning guns, and galley duty, he was now a trained specialist whose job was very much valued. Jack was bound and determined to thoroughly understand and practice all the ways to accurately forecast for navy air, land, and sea operations.

On July 22, 1937, Jack was assigned to the Aerological Office Naval Air Station, San Diego. His new duties included forecasting for VT-2 squadron (a photographic reconnaissance) operating out of San Diego. He also received pilot instruction under Lieutenant Danis. Flying a biplane in those days was quite the thrill and something Jack loved. He flew both a biplane with standard landing wheels and a pontoon biplane. He preferred landing on the ground because, as he often said, "The ground doesn't move!"

He learned to use instruments that monitor weather characteristics including temperature, air pressure, humidity, and wind speed and direction. He also became known as someone who could fix weather instruments that were not functioning properly.

Jack's duties included flying weather reconnaissance and the following:

–Direct weather information to ships and aircraft.

–Prepare balloon-carried instruments for flight, evaluating and analyzing all data.

–Collect, record, and analyze weather and oceanographic information.

–Prepare up-to-date weather maps and oceanographic data.

–Issue forecasts and warning information. Give written and oral weather briefings.

Jack's plane instructor

Jack was gaining invaluable responsibility and was on his way up in the navy.

Jack began going on bombing runs in a VT bomber at Camp Kearny, San Diego. This was a bombing range first used by the army and then by the navy and marines. It consisted of thousands of acres of land on which to practice bombing. He flew out to Camp Kearny for bomb soundings and to the Salton Sea for bombing practice. The Salton Sea was a desert bombing range in California. During this time, Jack reported in his journal that a lieutenant and an enlisted man crashed to death in bombing practice. The advent of air power to the armed forces was, at this stage, a very dangerous business.

In July 1937, Seaman First Class Ingram took the examination for third class petty officer. With hardly enough service to make it, he kept his fingers crossed. In the meantime he was assigned to USS *Lexington*, his first aircraft carrier while still being attached to VT-2 squadron. His duties included forecasting for all operations, in charge of aerograph soundings from the ship. Often, he would have battle station duties on the bridge and fly off the carrier for reconnaissance.

Jack seemed to enjoy his aerological work on USS *Lexington* because his job aboard a carrier was more challenging and more rewarding than the weather work associated with other surface ships. Carrier operations involved both seamanship and airmanship, and the weather had a great impact on both.

The weatherman's main duty on most surface ships was to advise the skipper of the weather he was going to encounter or avoid. Jack's duty aboard the *Lexington* was much more involved. Added to that main duty was the prospect of flying to take weather observations. Flying was, for any young man, a grand adventure, and it was thrilling for the young aerologist.

There were other aspects of carrier operations with biplanes that were more interesting, too. The *Lexington's* operations covered hundreds of miles. In other words, an air strike could be several hundred miles away. Conditions such as favorable or unfavorable winds all the way to the target and back affected fuel consumption, which had to be calculated. Also, the weather over the target could be much different from the weather over the carrier.

Weather balloons filled with helium were sent aloft and instruments such as a theodolite were used to determine wind speeds and directions at high altitudes, something extremely important to aircraft operations at sea.

Then there was the matter of launching and recovering aircraft. Both were more difficult in bad weather. If, for example, the weather was good when the ship launched an air strike against a target, it could be bad when the strike team returned, forcing the pilots to land on a pitching, yawing deck.

Another factor of air operations was that, in the early days of aircraft carriers, there had to be the right amount of wind over the deck to launch planes. Catapult launch capability had not yet been developed. Also, there was no radar or GPS (global positioning system) in the beginning of WWII to aid a pilot in locating his ship on the return flight. Radio signals were a pilot's friend, but inconsistent at best. As enormous as the carriers were at

USS *Lexington,* Jack's favorite image

USS *Lexington,* Diamond Head, Hawaii

that time, they were still awfully small compared to the vast ocean, and a lot of weather factors could affect a pilot or navigator's ability to find the ship. And, because flight missions often went great distances, fuel consumption was critical. If excessive time was spent looking for the ship, or if weather delayed landing, the pilots could run out of fuel and crash into the ocean.

At this time, Jack was anticipating achieving a rating of third-class aerographer. He hoped he would receive the promotion, and expected to be assigned duty on USS *Henderson*, sailing for Shanghai, China, where war raged between the Japanese and various elements of the Chinese Army ranging from the nationalist Chinese Army to the communist forces. It was a war that shocked the United States because the Japanese believed they were superior. Jack heard stories of the Japanese being unusually cruel to the Chinese who were unfortunate enough to fall under their swords.

USS *Lexington* combat squadron plane

September came, and the bureau had not sent orders. Jack did not go to the *Henderson*, nor did he get rated. Although it was a big disappointment because he had been rising quickly through the ranks, Jack resolved to work harder and keep trying. He took the exam for third class again, and he was ever hopeful. During this time, Jack started drawing commuter rations of $15.00 per month. Total month's pay was $69.00 less $4.00 insurance.

As December came to a close, Jack spent the holidays with his dad in town (San Diego). Jack enjoyed these reunions as he was now a bit more of a man of the world and a friend for his father, rather than their father-son relationship on the Rogue River.

By the first of the new year, Jack was still waiting for the results on his most recent test to become a 3rd class petty officer. Finally, the news of the results of his exam arrived in mid-February 1938. He exclaimed in his journal, "Hurray in a thousand lingos!! Praise God and thanks a million - I was rated third class petty officer! I am a fully qualified aerographer!!"

Though he was happy about his promotion, he did not rest easy. He set his sails for his next advancement. He wrote in his journal, "I will now be able to take examination for 2nd class before my first cruise is up. I'm expected to go to sea, any day now for spring maneuvers and Problem XIX."

During this period the navy had set war games called "Problems" that they practiced in pre-WWII years. Japan was always expected to be the enemy, so the maneuvers, at least from the navy's perspective, were based on defeating the Japanese Navy. There were many scenarios projected by the war department to test how U.S. forces would do against the Japanese at various expected flash points, such as Pearl Harbor in Hawaii, the Philippines, and the Aleutians. Unfortunately, they concluded wrongly that Pearl Harbor was too shallow an anchorage for a torpedo attack.

The Pacific fleet practiced constantly to counter Japanese strategies and possible attacks through a series of Problems. Jack's duty entailed making area forecasts for PBY (the abbreviation used to describe American patrol bombers) reconnaissance squadrons.

On the 5th of March 1938, Jack received orders to report to USS *Holland* for an Alaskan cruise. He was now senior aerographer of the watch.

US Navy sub in Dutch Harbor

He served as a forecaster on the *Holland* with two former shipmates, and now he had a stateroom for his office. He also gained experience on a submarine tender and even made dives in a sub. His ship was headed for Dutch Harbor, the main U.S. naval base in the Aleutian Islands.

On March 19, 1938, Jack arrived in Dutch Harbor and anchored. He had had a very rough passage; weather was characteristically unpredictable. These islands were the starkest panorama he had ever seen. Sharp pinnacles and peaks shot thousands of feet straight up until the summits were lost in the clouds. Pure and white, it was a virgin island. Dutch Harbor is situated on small Amaknak Island within the harbor of much larger Unalaska Island. Inilink Island was also visible from his anchorage. Jack noted in his journal, "Weather was swell and so was the fishing for cod, and flounder." The crew made sure the subs were being refueled and freshly provisioned. The weather forecast was for snow, snow, and more snow!

This assignment would become a center point of Jack's life and duty during World War II. The Aleutians had some of the worst weather in the world, and the living conditions there were harsh. For a weatherman, it provided the best meteorological experience one could get. The weather included rain, sleet, hail, snow, and fog. Sometimes all these conditions were encountered in the same day. Temperatures could fluctuate 40–50 degrees in a day!

In April, they were operating in Anderson Bay. Fox and eagles were plentiful, and the fish were easy to catch. Jack wrote in his journal, "The 'Williwaws' really kept us busy!" He later described a williwaw as a sudden blast of wind descending from a mountainous coast to the sea.

On April 7, he arrived at Chernofski Harbor to set up a meteorology station. Jack documented the arrival in his journal, "It's a treacherous harbor with poor protection. My ship was almost blown onto the rocks and there was plenty of excitement and thrills. All hands were on deck to protect the ship! Who could want more adventure?" Jack further documented in his journal, "On the 8th, I arrived at Akutan Harbor. From off shore, a cannery and an active volcano are in sight. It is an excellent harbor!"

Jack took part in one of the first photographic surveys for more advantageous submarine anchorages from Seattle to the Aleutians. He was learning photography by leaps and bounds and could now develop, print, and copy photos. Jack took all the shots he could of the barren land and surrounding waters in order to document future harbors for the Pacific fleet.

After his mission of finding and documenting good anchorages for the fleet, on April 15 Jack sailed for home. Two days later he celebrated three years in the U.S. Navy! And, he exclaimed in his journal, "Just a good start!" On April 24 he wrote that they had "tackled the last phase of our strategy problem." He also reported that on April 27 he had traveled 6,520 miles since his first sea duty in the navy.

Jack was careful about his finances. On May 1 he noted, "Made car payment and put $126.00 money in a Postal Service Account." It was important to him to stay current on payments, even when deployed.

On the 2nd of May, Jack reported back to duty at Long Beach, California, this time on board USS *Lexington.* Jack wrote, "I was thrilled with the *Lexington.* She was the largest carrier in the navy, 2200 men, 125 planes, with the most speed."

During the period from the 2nd to the 30th of May, he had Admiral's Inspections galore. Every man had to be clean, neat, and dressed in navy blues, standing at attention topside when the admiral inspected the crew.

Jack wrote, "What an outfit!" Even though Jack experienced his first biplane land on and take off from the deck, and watched a few planes crash, he was as thrilled with forecasting duties aboard the "Lady Lex" as he had been on his first assignment on USS *Pennsylvania.* Jack was now eligible for second class, which would increase his pay by twelve bucks a month. "Enough to do things with." On July 1, 1938, his ship arrived in Santa Barbara, California. Jack wrote, "I spent the Fourth of July in this beautiful little seacoast town."

Now that he was back aboard an aircraft carrier, Jack's duties differed a bit from the usual. Aircraft carriers and naval aviation were new to the navy in those days, and everybody involved was on a perpetual learning curve. There were frequent accidents due to the lack of experience, and they were still acquiring knowledge regarding aviation and aircraft carrier dynamics.

Aboard carriers, because wind was necessary for take-offs and landings, the flight deck could only use a certain wind envelope. The aerographer had to provide the wind direction and velocity, as well as the estimated amount of time that the commander could point the ship in the correct direction for planes to take off and land. They also needed to know the direction of the sea current because they had to contend with swells, which can be big rollers that rock the ship back and forth. Some operations would be postponed or canceled because of rough seas, and Jack's forecasts and briefings would help the captain with the start or stop command for flight operations.

Compared to land forecasters, aerographers at sea more frequently encountered the need to interpret unstable, frequently changing data. Because the ocean had a huge impact on the weather, forecasting at sea was both more dynamic and more difficult.

Many of Jack's classmates from Lakehurst were assigned to island duty, land-based weather stations in the western Pacific where they would radio weather information back to him so that a comprehensive forecast for operations could be understood.

Jack's job was not just necessary, but crucial. Yet, he still found time for the things that interested him, including his lifelong affinity for guns and shooting. On the 5th of July 1938, he put in for the pistol team. He bought a Colt .45 automatic pistol for $9.00. On the next day, he went to the pistol range at Wilmington and tried out for *Lexington*'s pistol team with Lieutenant Outerson. He had a lot of practice with his new Colt 45! Based on his

"Lady Lex" squadron planes

expertise with weapons, he had little trouble getting on the team and entered the Elysian P. Park matches and qualified as marksman.

At the same time, Jack was ambitiously moving things forward with his career. He reported in his journal that on the 29th of July, he was "put up for 2nd class." Being around planes on a carrier motivated him to continue his quest to keep flying, so in August of 1938, he put in a request for flight class at Pensacola, Florida. In mid-August he wrote, "I've had several crack ups on board. No injuries to personnel. Gruber did plenty of ribbing…a good natured, swell fellow. Ha-ha!" Flying a biplane definitely gave Jack an appreciation of the dynamics of carrier flights and the importance of offering detailed weather information for the captain to make safe, efficient, and effective flight operation decisions.

Jack went home on a three-day leave, and October 15 turned out to be an auspicious day for the young sailor. The *Lex* was in dry dock and, while stationed at the navy yard at Puget Sound, he met Doris Burns of Portland, Oregon. He marked the occasion with this simple, terse entry in his journal, "Met Doris Burns."

Although Doris was only sixteen, Jack was smitten with her. Their meeting had been fateful. Doris lived in an attic apartment above Jack's sister Mary's apartment, and she often spent time with "Aunt Mary" down in her living room. Doris had spotted Jack's photo on the fireplace mantel, so there was an obvious connection when she first met him. Jack didn't know it, but she had already fallen in love with the dashing young sailor in the photo.

Doris was one of two children in her family. Her older brother Bob was married and living close by in Portland. They had lost their parents two years prior. Doris and her brother were fortunate to have inherited money from the sale of a 2,000-acre parcel of land to the government in Pasco, Washington. This large tract of land was originally owned by Dora Buchanan Burns, who was the first non-native woman to have settled in Pasco; she and her husband Buchanan ran the first general store in town.

Doris, a quick-witted, thoughtful, and perceptive young woman, attended Portland's Polytechnic High School. She was also one of the first shoe models in Portland, Oregon. But her beauty extended above her feet and captured the young sailor's heart.

Although Doris was too young to marry at sixteen, the two made a pact. He was to go on an Asiatic cruise to the Philippines. When he returned, if they both still felt the same way, they would plan to be married.

Letters now became the chain that linked them, and her letters followed him to every ship and every duty station in the Pacific. The daily mail call, so familiar to all servicemen, took on a new and very special meaning now that Jack was anxiously awaiting letters from "his girl." Jack's pulse quickened each time there was a letter for him. It was the highlight of his day to take the letter, find a private place, and read it over and over again. An added thrill was when it was occasionally accompanied by a photograph which he could cherish and sneak peeks at during his day. Jack pined for her and dreamed of her with an ardor reserved only for those deeply in love.

Although Jack typically kept his journal entries quite professional, he began recording thoughts and events from the letters from Doris. Though he didn't put the specific words in his journal, he was in love. Now he hoped more than ever that she would still be available when he

Doris Burns was 16 in this photo. She gave it to Jack when he went off to the Philippines

Jack's navy photo that Doris loved

returned from the Philippines. After all, he thought, a young sixteen-year-old girl surely would not want to sit at home pining for a sailor boy who may or may not be as serious as he claimed to be about her. So, his journal entries became more centered on his new love. He wrote, "Doris is real sensible, so young. Swell girl. My girl!"

Obviously, his mind was on Doris much of his time. Finally, in November, he proposed to her. The two of them agreed that they would be married as soon as he returned from the Asiatic cruise. "Hot dog! She is lovely." Doris used to say, "Jack, don't change your life for me, but know that I'll be waiting for your return."

Soon after, on November 14, Jack was transferred to USS *Nitro* for further transfer to USS *Henderson*, for voluntary duty in the Asiatic fleet, the duty he had hoped for the previous year. USS *Nitro* was a U.S. Navy ammunition ship—not a very safe place to be stationed. Aboard the Nitro he wrote, "I miss Doris very much… Little sleep." "I should never have left her— I love her so darn much."

He reported on board U.S.S *Henderson* at Mare Island Naval Ship Yard, in Vallejo, California. On November 28 he sailed for Honolulu, territory of Hawaii. And, on December 3, he cruised for Guam in the Marshall Islands. Jack wrote in his journal, "Weather was a wee-bit rough for first three days! But since leaving Hawaii, you couldn't ask for more favorable conditions, so 'Sumpios,'" Jack's slang for wonderful. He went on to say, "I wish my two and a half years would fly by! Still, I've so much to learn. Why was man made so helpless?? I'll be home soon, Doris, soon… I pray to God she waits!"

Jack was a serious young man who was developing a life philosophy, something many people never do, no matter what their age. Jack surely was maturing in the navy. He did not seem to be the typical, carefree sailor. He had important responsibilities creating weather reports for operations at sea—always loyal to the navy's basic tenets of fidelity and obedience.

At a young age, he was already grounded with loyalty to his future wife and to the navy, unusual for a sailor still in his early twenties.

Jack's fourth great leadership character trait was *loyalty*!

Chapter Five

Philippines

Jack's First arrival in the Philippines - 1938

Every sailor who considers himself "salty" wants an Asiatic tour under his belt, and Jack was no exception. But he had another, more personal, reason for being happy about going to the Philippines. He needed it for promotion and more income, and the additional money was tied to his wish to go home and marry Doris Burns.

Jack was ambitious, adventurous, romantic, a good friend, and well-rounded. In some ways, he was typical of the ideal for his generation, an All-American young man. He was beginning to map out his future, which included a navy career, a beautiful wife named Doris, and a big family. But first things first, he had an Asian tour ahead of him.

Jack continued to record his travels in his journal. From December 7–10 he added several entries, "Royal Golden Dragon Crossed 180th meridian at 2400, 7 December, 1938. Initiated today the 10th Dragon Back—Most 'Wonderful' cruise I've ever had."

Before sailing to the Philippines, Jack's ship spent time in Guam. While in Guam he had an opportunity to observe the efficiency of the Pan Am Clipper, which was the long-range aircraft of its time and the precursor of international air travel. He noted that "The pilots have a responsible job."

By December 17, he was sailing to Manila, Philippine Islands, from Guam, Marianna Islands. By Christmas of 1938, he was at the receiving station at Cavite, Philippine Islands, where he further observed, "Manila is historical, hot, and interesting in extremes."

Jack with his Colt .45 pistol in the Philippines

He was enthralled with Far East sunsets and he related to his journal, "I have experienced the most beautiful sunsets I've ever seen, here in these tropical isles." He also added, "Typhoons and earthquakes occur frequently!"

On January 1, 1939, Jack started the new year by taking the examination for promotion to petty officer second class. His grade on the exam was 3.74 out of 4.00. On the 16th of January 1939, he reported, "No mail from home as yet." Finally, in late January, Jack received his first letter from Doris since the cruise started. He was both relieved and elated.

During this time, Jack was transferred by Commander Anderson to Radio Control Cavite for duty. Although Jack loved sea duty, it was nice to be back on land for a while. He bought a motorcycle for $40.00. He wrote, "What better way to get around these islands!" His naval career kept advancing. He was becoming ready to stand watch on the Asiatic weather broadcast.

On the 10th of February 1939, he started his first watch as weather dispatcher. He also joined the Cosmopolitan Gun Club where he kept his expert gun handling skills sharp alongside Admiral Yarnell, Admiral Hart, General MacArthur, and other superior officers. His navy duties included forecasting for Patrol Wing Ten, or PAT WING TEN, flying patrols in PBY float planes, forecasting for the western Pacific ships at sea. He set up the first weather observation posts on the eastern coast of the island of Luzon. These stations became of vital importance before, during, and after WWII, and it was a great responsibility for Jack.

New Boeing Clipper taking off in Philippines

The Philippines were relatively wild back in 1939 and setting up a weather station in these remote areas was an adventure. Jack's PBY reconnaissance weather observation flights included the southern tip of Formosa (now Taiwan) southward to Borneo. He was also given additional duty as second gunner using a .50-caliber mounted gun on those flights with PAT WING TEN.

Sometimes, Jack found himself on board USS *William B. Preston* or USS *Childs* forecasting at sea. Other times he forecast from advanced land bases that he set up around the western Pacific for fleet operations. Lieutenants Knell and Denham, Jack's commanding officers, frequently turned to Jack when a new station needed to be built and equipped, and when aerographers needed to be set up and trained to man these stations. The fleet ship captains appreciated Jack's network of stations and personal weather reports that assured timely and accurate forecasts for operations.

Jack loved being a part of naval operation in the Far East and was always keen to observe what was going on around him. On the 2nd of March 1939, Jack wrote in his journal, "I watched an historic event as a Boeing Clipper left for Hong Kong out of the bay."

On March 15 he wrote, "I am 22 years old today. I met Harmonantiz, head of Manila Weather Observatory Base. I also met Father Doucet, Father Deppermann, and Father Rappi, seismologists at the observatory."

On April 12, 1939, at Cavite, Philippine Islands, Jack wrote, "In five more days, I will have served four full years in the U.S. Navy. I've requested to reenlist for four more years." Jack was recommended for a good conduct medal and he received his Honorable Discharge Certificate before reenlisting for another four years.

Jack's career advanced. By June of 1939, he was holding the senior job at Radio Cavite in the Philippine Islands. His job involved forecasting and handling weather broadcasts for the Pacific fleet from the Philippine Asiatic Station. He based all his forecasts on daily weather information collected from aerologists serving on remote

Jack with Father Deppermann (World's Typhoon Expert)

island stations around the western and northern Pacific, as well as from aerologists flying on reconnaissance flights or sailing on ships at sea. All his forecasts were relayed to Weather Central at Pearl Harbor and to San Francisco as well. He had a lot of responsibility for such a young navy aerographer.

Jack wrote in his journal of a long talk he had with a Filipino boy, "Tony." Jack wrote, "He explained to me the hate of the true Filipino for Quezon, their President. Their language out here is called Tagalog. He was born in Bulacan (Boolikan) and looks more like a Japanese. It is not uncommon in this land, all races interbreed and the results are mestizos. Here in Cavite (Kaveete) are found natives from Batangan (Batungus), Tayabas (Tayibus), and Manila (Mansela.) Also, the barrio name Laguna has its representatives here. Santos, the oldest house boy finished the 7th grade and was able to enlist in the Insula Forces here. Tony finished the 5th and Nick the 4th. Tony was engaged at 7 years and married at 16, has a baby boy making him proud father at 18. Nick has 2 sons. Their average salaries are $20.00 per month. So, they manage to exist. A venereal-diseased native is usually murdered or exiled from the barrio. The government will not care for them, especially the poor."

As he matured, Jack became more philosophical, and his character gained dimension. In June of 1939, in line with his serious approach to life from Cavite, Philippines, he wrote, "In memoriam: All my travels have given me as a distinct realization, the truth and finality of death. When it was the lot of my loved one, to lose life's dearest possession, a mother, it caused anguish I could not then, or now express. Please, God, protect Doris. Always, now."

Jack was always thinking of Doris. On the 26th of November 1939, from Cavite, Philippine Islands, he wrote, "Have been engaged to Doris for one year and fourteen days today." He couldn't help but count the days. He did, however, find time to have some fun. He reported to his journal, "Learning to play tennis, bowl, and play bridge."

In December 1939, Jack was ordered to Manila by Commander Oates to work with Fathers Deppermann and Doucet of the Manila Observatory along with a full shore patrol. Jack's primary responsibility was to forecast weather throughout the western Pacific and create typhoon warnings for the fleet. He was now in charge of two other navy aerologists.

During this time, he wrote, "The European War that started 3 September between Germany, France, and England has now involved Russia and Finland. Canada and Australia are in, too, and the conflict between Japan and China, continues." In the back of his mind, he knew that all hell was going to break loose with Japan because of the reports, stories, and personal encounters he experienced throughout the islands.

One personal adventure he discussed in his journal encompassed taking a trip of about ten kilometers up a small river north of Manila. He said, "The stream was full of fish life, clams, and mussels. All along the stream were grass and bamboo huts. Curious natives watched from the shore. Plenty of bolos (knives) were in evidence. Our boat drew about 3 feet of water, counting the length of the outboard motor shaft for the prop. Motor died on us up in the headwaters and we had to row on to the end of the navigable waters. The stream empties into Bacoor Bay and the headwaters begin in the vicinity of Tagaytay Ridge. It was an enjoyable trip having spent one entire day making it. P.S. Had .45 pistol along!" Jack liked to carry his pistol in these scenarios, comparing himself to a Wild-West character in dangerous territory. It appealed to his sense of adventure. The Philippines was not exactly a totally "civilized" place back in the thirties, and many bandits still roamed the countryside.

On the 16th of February, from Cavite Jack wrote, "Good career news— I was advanced to petty officer second class and aerographer!!!" He was thrilled with this promotion, as with his others, and it made him even more determined to work hard and continue to advance. Yet even with his hard work, he continued his hobbies and sports, and even started a stamp collection.

Jack was advancing quickly within the ranks of the navy. In his journal, he wrote, "As an aerographer my duties have involved prolonged cruises through the China Sea, Zula Sea, Celebes Sea, from Tawi and Zamboanga to Manila and Hong Kong. I have stood junior officer of the deck watches in port, signal and quartermaster watches, in addition to special duty of forecasting from advanced bases on terminal (land) and route (sea) weather."

Life in prewar Philippines continued. On the 17th of February, Jack mentioned in his journal, "Admiral Smallie invited the U.S. army post from Baguio to bring down two companies of Igorots to entertain us with their native dances. The men wore G strings made of brilliant colors to attract the women. They all carried bolos, 18 to 24 inches long and spears pointed on both ends. "B" Company wore bracelets on arms and legs, they were the Ifugao tribe. The other "A" Company called Bontoc had a brass circular drum about 10 inches in diameter. This was the only music they had to keep rhythm. The dances were all similar and consisted of spasmodic jerks or motions not unlike some of our own jitterbug type of dancing. The women were all fully clothed, it is not the custom however."

In another insightful journal entry Jack wrote, "To me, it is inconceivable how any married man can cheat on his wife and yet some of these dumber sorts out here, that call themselves servicemen, a far-fetched presumption in my opinion, make it a common and cheap practice. No ideals I know of harbor such actions. I'm no angel but by all that's holy and sacred to me if I were to take a wife it will be for all time, unending. Course I'm just a kid, but some of us have ideals you know."

During this time, Jack always thought of Doris and how he would conduct himself if only she could wait for him to return. His journal on April 17 read, "I'm sure now that I love her. Fingers crossed." On one of Jack's journeys to Hong Kong, he met a wood carver who carved an elm-wood hope chest lined with cedar for Doris. The chest exhibited beautiful hand carvings on its entire surface that depicted a love story. He couldn't wait to bring the chest back and give it to Doris.

Jack was eager about flying, and he wrote in his journal that he flew to 11,000 feet off USS *Langley* aircraft carrier. Jack was now assigned to the *Langley* and still serving as a chief forecaster for PAT WING TEN in the Philippines. While on USS *Langley*, Jack had three navy aerologists assigned to him. Jack reported all his forecasts directly to Admiral Harry Yarnell and later to Admiral Thomas Hart; both were commanders of the Asiatic fleet. Yarnell and Hart were veterans of the Spanish-American War. Like old Crowe from the Rogue, they had their stories to tell!

In May, Jack was excited about Doris sending a picture. He wrote, "Gee, she is adorable!" But Jack's elation was tempered by the events happening in the world. "The hideousness of modern warfare is today being realized in practically every country, nation, or republic in Europe. The swiftness of the 'blitzkrieg' is astounding. It is strange how a man like Hitler who is striving so hard to conquer this world, can so completely ignore the truth of God who says, 'Seek ye first the Kingdom of God.'" In a pensive mood he wrote, "What doth it profit a man if he gains the whole world and suffers the loss of his own soul? I hope America will not have to stop him. Time will tell!"

A dire prediction makes the pages of Jack's journal on the 21st of June: "Cavite. Philippines Islands. I have received instruction in new small arms usage again. We will fire them before long. France has given in to Germany. Belgium and Holland gave in several weeks ago. War! War! War!"

Bill Ingram racing at Silvergate race track

Bill Ingram – Midget car racer

On August 15, 1940, Jack had a sad event to record in his journal. He wrote, "William (Bill) Frank Ingram. My brother. Two years high school. Apprentice under his Dad. Bill who was an auto body man, fenders man, first class mechanic, first superintendent of Buick Motor Company, San Diego, California was injured at Balboa race track in midget racer and died due to 7 crushed vertebrae, multiple fractures of both arms, broken leg, fracture of skull, never regained consciousness. Mary Stewart said he was driving his car right to the end. My Dad flew to San Diego and brought Bill back to Portland. He was buried in Verboort, Oregon. He was 27, died in the Quintard Hospital. Bill Zaring skidded into Bill Ingram forcing him into the crash wall. Bill Ingram was pinned beneath and dragged by his overturned racer. He is survived by Alice, Walter, and Arlene Ingram. It was on a Wednesday night that he was racing in the main event. Someday, I'll be able to check up on this Bill Zaring and find out just what had actually happened."

Jack took his brother's death hard, although he didn't have the words to express his feelings. He found himself reduced to a flat obituary-type statement about Bill's death for the time being. Although he was stoic about the obituary, he kept many mementos of his brother and his career in auto racing.

Among the things he saved was a local newspaper account of the crash and Bill Ingram's death:

"When Bill Ingram was faced with the problem that must come to every racing driver—the problem of weighing his life against the lives of others—in a lightning fast decision he took the hero's way out. But, if that decision was made in a fraction of a second it was the result of a character that he built up through all the years of his life. Honest, sincere, loyal, courageous. . . ."

Jack kept this clipping throughout his life. It said it better than he could have said it himself. He was very proud of his big brother Bill and had a stronger case of big-brother idolization than most other younger brothers. That was likely because Bill was involved

Bill and Jack Ingram together in Portland

in something that roused a young boy's imagination: *he was a fearless midget-race car driver!*

The character of American racing involved love of speed first. Then there was the undeniable visceral appeal of the roar of high-performance engines straining and competing against each other. Bill Ingram would travel to Detroit once a year to buy a new car to procure the newest engine. He would then bore out the engine block and fabricate and install larger pistons in an effort to find an edge. So, when Jack talked about family with others, he boasted about Bill's exploits on the racetrack. Jack kept all the newspaper accounts of his races.

One race he never forgot was at the Silvergate Speedway. It was Bill's first race, a 140-lap stock car event watched by 2,500 fans. For 120 laps Bill ate the dust of Joe Wilbur and Bud Rose. Wilbur held the lead for 120 laps. When Wilbur went into a spin on the last lap, Bill passed him to win through the clouds of dust, which hampered many of the drivers on the turns. As it turned out, Bill delivered one of the best performances ever seen at Silvergate Speedway. Jack was always up to date with Bill's entire racing history!

Despite his grief over the loss of his big brother, Jack continued making impressive advances in the navy. On the 6th of November 1940, from Cavite, Philippine Islands, Jack took the examination for aerographer first class, and he believed he would receive a passing mark. Indeed, he made petty officer first class (aerographer first class) on November 16. He was now rated for civilian clothes privileges and his monthly pay increased from (base pay) $72.00 to $84.00 plus 10% or $92.40. Ever ambitious, on April 8, 1941, he requested Advanced Aerographic School for chief. His request was approved! He had accomplished his goal: advance in rating enough to marry Doris Mae Burns!

Time passed quickly and by September 1941, Jack was in Manila and still attached to Squadron PAT WING TEN. He was flying more and more PBY reconnaissance flights—setting up additional weather stations for the Pacific fleet throughout the western Pacific. He gained invaluable experience forecasting for Pacific storms and typhoons! During this time, he always thought that war was on the horizon.

In addition to being attached to PAT WING TEN, Jack also had forecasting assignments on USS *William B. Preston* and he acknowledges the following staff of his ship:

"Lt Comdr. F. J. Bridges, Capt. Lt L.O. Wood, Ens. Lt (j.g.) McLaren, Engineer Lt (j.g.) Slight, 1st Lieut. Ens. Kriloff, Communications Off. Ens. Holcombe, USNR Mason, SM 1/c Steves, SM 3/c Masa, COM McGinty, QM 1/c Ingram, Aerog 1/c Noble, Sea 1/c Flanders, FC 3/c Pacquet, Sea 1/c Pieck, AOM 3/c Rose, GM 3/c Farnham, GM 1/c Atwell, BM 1/c O'Brien, BM 2/c Weyant, Cox. Benderman, CEM Vandewalker, QM 1/c USNR. Price, CBM USNR. Cooper, Yeo 1/c Bruner, Yeo 2/c Watson, EM 1/c Little, EM 2/c Salenski, Sea 1/c Vibert, Sea 1/c Yeynon (Dee), Phmc 1/c Goodrum, CM 1/c Robertsen, SF 3/c MacMahon, F 1/c Law, SC 1/c"

Jack's primary job aboard USS *Preston* was to forecast for ship operations at sea and at an advanced base island terminal. In his journal, Jack listed the ships he had been on since leaving USS *Henderson*: USS *Childs*, USS *Langley*, USS *William B. Preston*, USS *Bulmer*, USS *Heron*, and USS *Marblehead*.

Later he wrote in his journal, "By some miraculous power, I got orders home to the U.S., left Sangley Point on Oct 1, 1941. On the USS *Guadalupe* oil tanker, transferred at sea in the inland waters of the Philippines, San Bernardino Strait, to the cruiser USS *Phoenix* and USS *Albemarle*. Arrived Pearl Harbor Oct 20, 1941. Departed Pearl Harbor on the USS *Oglala* in October." October 27, 1941, he jubilantly wrote, "Left for the U.S.!" On November 1, 1941, Jack arrived at the Golden Gate Bridge . . . home!

His Asiatic adventure was over, and Jack looked forward to a new phase of his life. His time in the Philippines had given him a sense of the world beyond the borders of the United States. He had also developed a strong feeling of empathy for other cultures around the Pacific that were being invaded and exploited by the Japanese. During this time, he felt like the very order of things around the world was unstable and at great risk.

Jack by this time in his life had formed a stable path for himself. He had decided on the principles he would live by as he related in the following early journal notation: "Five Duties Line Each Mortal Path that Leads to Life's Far Border—To Live, To Learn, To Serve, To Earn, To Set One's House in Order."

Jack's fifth great leadership character trait was *stability*!

Chapter Six
World War II

Seasoned navy aerographer Jack Ingram was thrilled to find that Doris still felt the same way about him. The long, lonely months in the Philippines and at sea were over at last. Now the two could fulfill their dreams born of countless letters, and they began planning their wedding. The Chinese hope chest helped to seal the deal!

On November 22, 1941, twenty-four-year-old Jack Ingram married eighteen-year-old Doris Mae Burns. Father John Margraf officiated a Catholic wedding at Our Lady of Sorrows in Portland. Their marriage occurred at that very point in history when America was, in two weeks, about to face its biggest challenge to date, World War Two, a global conflict that was to be fought in two major theaters. And there was no doubt that, at least in the Pacific, it was going to be a navy war, as someone put it, "A gut-busting navy war."

Chinese chest carved in Hong Kong for Doris

Wedding picture of Jack and Doris

During the Japanese attack on December 7, 1941, USS *Pennsylvania* was in dry dock in the Pearl Harbor Naval Shipyard. She was one of the first ships to open fire at Japanese dive bombers attempting to bomb and strafe the ship. Some of Jack's former gun crew of his five-inch broadside battery were wiped out when a bomb struck the starboard side of the boat deck and exploded inside. He never forgot his buddies who lost their lives that day.

Back then, many young Americans, including Jack and Doris, were naïve and even innocent in some ways. They clung to the prevailing culture, an ardent love of family, home, and country evidenced by the long lines of young men in front of the recruiting offices the day after Pearl Harbor, ready to volunteer for a war. It was a war that they had no idea would be brutal and horrific beyond what they could ever imagine.

The newlyweds were assigned to Navy Weather Central at San Francisco, California. Both Jack and Doris were thrilled that his first assignment after their wedding was a shore-based job, meaning Jack would not have to ship out to some faraway place. San Francisco was a romantic place, perfect for a newly married young couple. They enjoyed the area and spent every spare moment together. Looming over them, however, was the constant concern that Jack would soon be called to war.

Jack was serving under Commander Wilbur M. Lockhart. At the time, Commander Lockhart was the navy's most senior weatherman reporting to Admiral Chester Nimitz. Jack's duties at the San Francisco Navy Fleet Weather Central (Com Twelfth Naval District) involved gathering weather information from many sources, including Pearl Harbor, land-based island weather stations throughout the Pacific, and Father Deppermann's weather observatory in the Philippines. Incidentally, Jack's friend, Father Deppermann, had become recognized as the world's leading expert on weather and typhoons in the Pacific.

After accumulating information and weather data, Jack forecasted and transmitted comprehensive weather reports to the Pacific fleet for planning operations against the Japanese. Jack had a network of thirty-eight transoceanic navy aerographer forecasters in the Pacific theater of operations reporting to him from air, land, and sea. Jack reported directly to Lockhart who reported to Admiral Nimitz.

In San Francisco, weather reports and weather warnings were filed and transmitted every six hours giving at least a twenty-four- to forty-eight-hour warning to all ships and aircraft at sea in the Pacific theater of war.

Tracking typhoons was especially interesting. The aerographers would track the range and bearing of the eye of the storms based on all data and reports. In addition to the thirty-eight forecasters reporting to him, Jack had strong ties with other aerologists collecting weather data in the Pacific from land-based stations, ships, and airplane reconnaissance patrols. They relied on each other to generate accurate and meaningful forecasts for operations. Because Jack had set up many of the Pacific island land-based weather stations, he had a special bond with his navy aerographer friends assigned to those stations.

As the war progressed Jack occasionally received bad news that the Japanese had captured one of the stations that he had set up. Jack felt terrible about the buddies who were captured or lost when the weather

Newlywed couple

stations were taken. He grieved for those who were killed, but he did not want to imagine what happened to those who survived the attacks and were captured by the Japanese.

Interestingly, the Japanese would often keep the weather stations working and would transmit information using the U.S. land-based radios. The U.S. intercepted the transmissions and these intercepts were some of the first navy intelligence used to spy on the Japanese during the war. Jack's navy aerographer buddies were the first to realize the Japanese activity, interpret the broadcasts, and report them back to Nimitz. These early intercepts helped the U.S. fleet to safely plan missions at sea in the beginning of the war.

Later, Japanese forces became more sophisticated and stopped using U.S. equipment, but navy intelligence was able to crack their codes, and aerographers were given dual roles with forecasting and listening responsibilities, becoming some of the first U.S. navy intelligence personnel in the Pacific.

Fleet Admiral Chester Nimitz had the highest respect for navy aerographers and appreciated the briefings that Commander Lockhart's team, including Jack and his colleagues, produced around the clock from San Francisco Navy Fleet Weather Central.

In early August of 1942, Jack took the examination for chief petty officer—chief aerographer and, on October 1 of the same year, he was appointed to chief petty officer of the U.S. Navy.

A few months later, on October 15, 1942, Doris and Jack became the parents of an eight-pound, one-ounce baby girl, Karen Marie Ingram. Both were as happy and proud as any new parents could possibly be. But Doris had experienced a very difficult labor and the doctor warned her that she should not have any more children. The news was devastating to Jack and Doris, but they didn't dwell on it because their joy for their new baby filled their lives.

While Jack and Doris were settling into their family life, Jack's dad, Earl, was asked to return to his boilermaker job and run the union in Portland. Even though ship building was robust again, Earl never gave

Newly minted Navy Chief Petty Officer

up his gold claim on the Rogue. He continued to split his time between Portland and searching for the "mother lode" of gold on the Rogue.

On November 22, Jack and Doris celebrated their first wedding anniversary. Jack now knew that an Alaska and Aleutian Island assignment was in view, but such information was kept secret. When Japanese Admiral Yamamoto, the architect of the Pearl Harbor sneak attack, planned his conquest of Midway Island, he included a feint toward the Aleutians. This had two purposes. First, of course, was to deceive the Americans as to the real target. But also, after the Doolittle raid—a morale buster for the Japanese nation—they wanted to gain a foothold on American soil and thus put Japan back onto a path to victory. Also, Yamamoto thought that this would prevent America from launching an invasion against Japan from the Aleutians.

While the Battle of Midway turned out to be a disaster for the Japanese Navy, they did manage to establish a foothold on the Aleutian Islands of Attu and Kiska. Unfortunately, U.S. forces did not have the resources to prevent the Japanese occupation. The Japanese were essentially unopposed! Aerographer Charles House's daily forecasts from Kiska Island to his friend Jack and Fleet Central ended.

House, a fellow Navy aerographer and close friend of Jack's, was eventually captured by Japanese soldiers after holding out for forty-nine days alone on Kiska. His adventures in doing so became legendary.

House hid from the Japanese eating worms and grubs to stay alive. He also was hidden and helped by three local native Aleut friends. After fainting one morning, he eventually surrendered to stay alive. Japanese troops captured him and threw him into the forward hold of Japanese transport ship. He eventually departed on the *Nagata Maru* destined for POW camps in Japan.

Forty-three Aleuts were transported to POW camps in Japan along with Charlie. They slept on tatami mats and subsisted on fish heads and small quantities of rice. They were malnourished and struggled to survive.

Meanwhile, Japanese forces occupied and fortified Attu and Kiska. The American people were outraged that the Japanese occupied American territory in North America. So in May, after the Battle of the Komandorski Islands opened a sea lane to Attu, the United States attacked with 11,000 troops from the north and south ends of the barren island.

Though there were only 2,500 Japanese defenders, they were acclimated and ready after spending a year digging into defensive positions. The Americans, on the other hand, expecting an offensive operation of only a couple of days, had substandard gear and inadequate clothing for the wet, freezing cold. There were as many American casualties from the weather as from the Japanese!

It took three weeks for the U.S. forces to clear Attu Island. In the end, the Japanese made desperate kamikaze attacks which failed. Most of the survivors, true to the ancient Samurai code of Bushido, killed themselves. Of 2,500 Japanese troops on the island, only 30 surrendered. Attu was back in American hands.

In August, the army landed on Kiska only to find that the Japanese forces had evacuated from the island. Now the U.S. Navy could commence bombing operations against the Japanese Kurile Islands chain.

The only consistent description of the weather in the Aleutians was "it was consistently bad" with only a brief period during the summer when it was reasonably stable. Generally speaking, the islands were cold, windy, foggy, and barren.

Before the age of pressurized aircraft, air crews, even in warmer climates, went out with their extra-heavy fleece- and fur-lined jackets, deerskin fur-lined gloves and boots, and, after thirteen-hour patrols, still came back half frozen. In the Aleutians, if one could imagine, it was even worse. One could freeze to death at night by walking unprotected to the latrine. One serviceman died tragically that way. Some aerographers, pilots, and crew members were fortunate to wear "flight skins." Skins were heavy, fur-lined, one-piece leather coveralls issued for reconnaissance and bombing missions.

Before Jack was assigned to forecast in the Aleutians, Commander Lockhart would say, "Aleutian weather has been widely publicized since the outbreak of the war in numerous newspapers and magazines, as well as on the radio. We have heard that the Aleutian Islands are the home of the largest 'Lows' of the northern hemisphere and that it is the breeding ground for the worst storms, gales, and perpetual fog.. . . . Well, it's all true!"

Jack's selection for this wartime theater came from high up the navy chain of command. Jack was selected by Commander Lockhart and Admiral Nimitz for a special task. It was to be his job to motivate men to fly, even in marginal weather. He knew that accurate aerological weather reports would take some of the danger out of encountering bad weather. Jack's job was to forecast for the best operational weather conditions and then motivate the men to fly based on his accuracy and consistency.

By September 15, 1943, Jack was a warrant officer. Jack's domain for part of the war would be forecasting to defend the Aleutian Islands with personal orders from Nimitz to "keep the planes in the air," referring to FLEET AIR WING FOUR, which was performing reconnaissance missions by day and bombing raids on Japan at night.

Of course, weather would become the most critical factor in planning, flying, bombing, and landing for a mission's success or failure. Jack did little to chronicle his wartime experience in the Aleutians because of ordered secrecy. A younger aerologist mate, Paul Carrigan, one of the twelve aerologists under his immediate supervision, did write about his experiences.

Jack reporting for Aleutian duty (Fleet Air Wing Four)

Young Paul Carrigan said, "Jack Ingram, warrant officer, arrived in Attu and reminded everyone that they all had to 'fly the weather,'" which was Jack's rendition of Nimitz's orders "to keep them in the air."

While in the Aleutians, Jack would serve directly under FLEET AIR WING FOUR Commander Leslie Gehres. Until Jack reported for duty, Gehres would frequently call "STOP" for air missions, for any sign of poor weather or perceived adversity. Both Lockhart and Nimitz knew that Jack's tested and contagious leadership would help to encourage Gehres to become more assertive with "GO" calls for bombing missions against the Japanese. One of the primary reasons for Jack Ingram's assignment to the Aleutians was not only because he had accurate operational forecasting experience with the fleet, but because Commander Lockhart and Admiral Nimitz knew that Jack Ingram was the man who could "keep them flying." Nimitz had come to understand the reliability of the fundamental correctness of Jack's empirical weather data and simple distillation of its delivery for operations.

Jack did not accomplish this mission with any sort of machismo but rather with the factual quality and integrity of his weather forecasting and briefings. In the past, vague weather reports did nothing to encourage operations. Jack improved forecasting so that Gehres could make better decisions. Jack was able to reduce anxiety by providing the CO and pilots with better reports. Rather than to succumb to bad weather, which was virtually constant, Jack instilled confidence in the

Heavy Patrol bombing Squadron One Hundred Thirty-Five (Jack is second from left)

pilots by forecasting the best weather—a tough thing to do with the bravest of airmen.

Jack also spent time on the remote Aleutian island of Amchitka. But it was from Attu that Jack flew the weather with the navy, launching some major raids against the Japanese Kurile Islands. The navy missions were held in great secrecy for most of the war until the United States started to greatly impact the Japanese strongholds. The press was not allowed to document or offer news about the operations, nor was Jack or his crew allowed to write home about them.

The Kuriles, the northernmost of the main Japanese islands, lie about 1,200 miles from Tokyo. The biggest Japanese naval base in the northern Pacific was Paramushiro in the Kuriles, and the U.S. Navy wanted to knock it out and keep the Japanese on their heels. Up until this point, the American strategy involved gaining bases in the western and central Pacific so that they could bomb Japan. The marines fought many bloody battles from Tarawa to Okinawa to secure bases. Now, the northern Pacific became important too.

Here, Navy aerographers like Jack had the tough job predicting "the unpredictable weather" so that the raids would not have the additional hazard of poor flying conditions for missions. Jack was familiar with air wing duties and operations from his forecasting duties before the war with both VT-2 squadron (1937) and PAT WING TEN (1941), but he now was responsible for lives in a wartime environment in which flyers ran the risk of being shot down.

As part of his extraordinary leadership, and as motivation to "keep them in the air," Jack often flew on missions to gain the trust of the pilots

Jack is standing on the right after a night mission

and crews that his forecasts were solid and safe for observations and for bombing over targets. On occasion, a rapidly changing weather pattern made forecasting with the available data even more difficult than usual. When possible under these conditions, a weather plane was sent out with Jack aboard as observer. The information obtained from direct observation, when tied together with other island and fleet reports, permitted more accurate weather analysis than would otherwise have been possible. The efficacy of Jack's job resulted in the success or failure of each mission and the life or death of many air crew members. Everyone knew that weather could kill more men than Japanese anti-aircraft guns and fighter aircraft.

Jack sometimes took part in bombing missions. On one such mission, his patrol bomber was on the homeward leg, normally a time full of relief for having survived another bombing operation. But not in the Aleutians. The biggest problem, as ever, was the weather and what it did to spartan WWII warplanes. The crew's new radar acted like it was frozen, and all that showed on the scope was one big "white fuzz ball." Making matters worse, their compass needle was sporadically jumping all over! The radio was intermittent and fading. To find their way back and get a fix on Attu's landing strip, Jack would have to take navigational

Fleet Air Wing Four PBY reconnaissance plane on Attu

star sightings. First, they had to get above the cloud layer, which was very high, and the temperature was even more frigid. With dwindling fuel and none to spare they climbed above the clouds. Jack was able to take a star sighting accurate enough to give them a heading for flying to their home base—back to the small landing strip on Attu Island.

By the time the airfield was in sight, the fuel situation was critical, and there was time only for one landing pass. They had to get it right. Every heart was beating hard, and all lips were murmuring their prayers as the crew caught sight of the runway. The ground crews lined the runway with fifty-five-gallon drums of fuel and set them afire. When finally the chirp and squeal of rubber was heard on the steel-grid runway, Jack's crew knew that the grace of God brought them home safely. Just another day flying in the Aleutians!

Life on these islands was bleak. And for everybody, especially married men, it was lonely. For the military personnel stationed there, there was no break, no relief with liberty in San Diego or "Frisco" with their bars, hotels, and fine restaurants, something that all servicemen often considered a necessity to relieve the stress and horror of war.

The barren, cold, and windswept islands were bereft of any trees. Aleutian vegetation consisted of shallow-rooted bearberry, heath, sedges, mosses, and lichen growing on an icy tundra. Relief was the far-too-brief Aleutian summer when beautiful wildflowers bloomed, and patches of native grasses emerged, as the tundra soil thawed a few inches on top of the perpetual ice beneath.

During the very short summer, Jack was happy when Commander Gehres gave him a fun present in the form of a dairy cow shipped from the west coast. Half joke and half practicality, Jack knew how to take care of the "milk machine" from what he had learned as a kid back on the Jansen farm, and everyone appreciated his ability to look after the animal. Fresh milk and ice cream for all!

What passed for recreation happened in Quonset huts and in a large, warm, wood-framed recreation hall. Here an off-duty man could relax, have coffee and other refreshments, play cards or board games, write letters home, and listen to music on the jukebox. This jukebox music included tunes like the rollicking "Don't Sit Under the Apple Tree" in which a GI asks his girl not to "sit under the apple tree with anyone else but me, anyone else but me, anyone else but me, no, no, no, don't sit under the apple tree with anyone else but me Till I come marching home."

Another popular tune was the sentimental and heart wrenching, "I'll Be Seeing You" "in all the old familiar places, That this heart of mine embraces All day through." Evenings also brought the diatribe of Tokyo Rose, who would broadcast sarcastic rumors and innuendo about the U.S. military over the radio.

Then there was the dance craze of the day back home, the jitterbug, inspired by such numbers as "The Boogie Woogie Bugle Boy." There were times when such songs couldn't keep dancing feet still and groups of men broke out into jitterbugging with each other with all the latest moves, dips, and acrobatics.

Because of the security black out, it was hard to candidly write home about what anyone was experiencing. All that any of Jack's family at home knew was that Jack was forecasting weather for operations against the Japanese somewhere in the Pacific.

Living conditions and recreation facilities eventually improved greatly at Amchitka. The enlisted personnel built their own beautiful beer hall, the Golden Dragon. USO troupes toured the Aleutians more often and Bud Freeman and his U.S. Army band and Tommy Tucker's band visited Amchitka.

Of course, like aboard ship, there were movie nights, when a man could lose himself in a Zane Grey Western being portrayed on the screen. He could forget his troubles and become immersed in Hollywood's latest offering and feel somewhat like he was back home.

Duty was a daily grind in these dismal islands. The sequence of weather in the northern Pacific was complicated and the controlling factors complex; any attempt to show the relationship between them would be inordinately lengthy. The Aleutian weather for the time period was summarized in Jack's papers:

Cow given to Jack from Gehres

"A front extended across the route between Amchitka and Paramushiro partially each month from January to part of the month of May. The influence of weather associated with a front south of the route and extending across the route or over the terminals was felt, again partially, during the months of December through May. Winds of over 25 knots prevailed in the area even in the absence of fronts or frontal weather 25% of December, 35% of January and February, 28% of March, and 26% of April, from there it began to diminish."

Jack's aerological data from Attu from December 1943 to May 1944 were studied to determine the nature of the weather at FLEET AIR WING FOUR's base. His following definitions were used for analysis:

"-Air base closed for operations when visibility is less than one mile and ceiling less than 1,000'.

"-Flying conditions are unfavorable when ceiling is less than 1,000 feet, visibility is less than 2 ½ miles, or surface wind 20 knots or greater."

Jack and his fellow aerographers had to figure out acceptable plans for flying conditions to and from targets. One thing to understand about flyers in this theater, or any other war zones, was that nobody was a draftee. All of the flyers were volunteers! In some of the worst flying conditions on the planet, it was understandable how a man might be impatient to go on missions. In the flying services, a flight surgeon or CO could ground any man, not because he was sick or unable, but because he might be too jittery to fly.

Commander Gehres, Jack's CO, had severe personal inhibitions about flying in the Aleutians. But Jack lived to forecast for missions and to fly the missions he forecasted, instilling confidence in Gehres's mission "GO" calls and his fellow Navy aviators. With the best forecast possible and with an aerographer like Jack on board, they knew the flight mission route should be safe and successful!

Jack's weather briefs were very descriptive and helped to inspire flight crews to better understand what kind of weather they would encounter on reconnaissance or bombing missions. An excerpt from one of Jack's weather briefings read:

"A storm frontal area, with unfavorable flying weather along the projected route will be encountered, and it is narrowly defined. This zone will be no more than 80 miles in width and will be moving eastward with a velocity of 18–22 miles per hour. A few cumuli generating snow showers should give moderate icing but not detrimentally affect flight in the frontal zone and along the remainder of the route if flight is sustained at 8,000 to 10,000 feet. Visibility over the target area will be unrestricted. On the return route, a temperature inversion and vertical development of high emerging layers of alto cumulus and stratus over 10,000 feet could create unstable flight. Note: Flying between 8,000 and 10,000 feet along the desired route should ensure the success of the entire mission."

Jack's forecasts and briefings for bombing missions served to give an increased layer of confidence to Commander Gehres. After understanding the weather risks and benefits, Gehres would then make the "GO" call for bombing missions, which gave the navy flyers solace of mind, inspiring them to focus on the Japanese targets instead of the weather, especially knowing that Jack often flew with them.

Commander Gehres wrote, "The pilots trusted the aerologists and had confidence in their predictions. Their trust was engendered by the aerologist's incurable habit of flying with pilots through their own predicted weather and the repeatedly proved accuracy of their forecasts. The weathermen had the confidence in their own work which comes with long study, careful tabulation, and recording of long-gathered data and thorough analysis of all the elements involved."

After the war, Jack and Gehres coauthored a classified publication named "Aerology and Naval Warfare – FLEET AIR WING FOUR STRIKES." The document was requested by the Chief of Naval Operations.

Jack's sixth great leadership character trait was *inspiration*!

Personal photo of Gehres given with a note: To Jack Ingram, Aerographer weather advisor to the "Empire Night Express" Well done!

Chapter Seven

Empire Express: "Fly the Weather"

Every theater of operations came up with its own nickname during the war. In the South Pacific, it was the "Tokyo Express" to Guadalcanal. In the Aleutians, it was first the "Tokyo Short Line Express," then the "Empire Night Express," and later it was shortened to "Empire Express." The reason for the name change was that missions went from happening under the cloak of darkness to daytime hours. Missions became more and more successful because bombing crews had learned to both avoid poor weather and hide behind cloud layers and storm fronts as they flew to and from Japanese targets. Weather had become a tactical advantage!

Sector patrols for Navy PV-1 Ventura planes out of Attu varied and usually meant flying into Japanese territory. The PV-1 Ventura made it possible for the air wing to continue its role of carrying the war to Japan's Kurile Islands and "keeping the Japs on their heels." Instead of the Aleutians being a Japanese pathway to Alaska and the west coast of Canada and the United States, they became the U.S. forces' stepping stones to Japan, and Attu was the closest "rock." Accurate weather information en route and over the target area was so vital that a special early-morning, high-altitude PV-1 weather reconnaissance mission to Paramushiro was scheduled daily regardless of whether a bombing mission was scheduled for that night. As a result, aerographers on Attu were ordered to fly in PV-1s to the Kurile target areas. A second aerographer's mate was often sent in a PBY to search out a front or storm center in a more northwesterly or southern sector. Weather information gathered by the aerographer's mates on the early-morning Paramushiro mission—"the milk run" (as consistent as a "milkman" delivering milk from the "gifted cow")—determined whether a scheduled night bombing strike by PV-1s should be mounted or canceled. Many days the weather flight "milk run" was flown but the bombing mission scrubbed because the weather was deemed too bad. PBYs flew regular, long, sector searches that fanned out from Attu, and PV-1s flew bombing missions.

Information provided by day and night photographic/bombing missions always produced surprises. U.S. Naval Intelligence had known for many years that Paramushiro Island was a large Japanese naval base, staging area, and sortie point for Japan's northern naval fleet. The Japanese navy's land-based, long-range Mitsubishi planes, named "Bettys," made their Aleutian raids from island airfields in the vicinity. But the extent of Japanese installations came as a surprise. FLEET AIR WING FOUR's aerial strikes on Kurile installations, carried out by a handful of PV-1 Venturas operating in guerilla fashion, made a tremendous contribution by keeping pressure on Japan, forcing them to constantly divert a substantial percentage of a struggling economic war effort to the north.

In his journal, Jack described a flight with VPB Bomber Squadron 139, near the time of his birthday in March 1944. His air crew had a successful bombing raid on Kurabu Zaki Island, where they bombed Japanese ships and installations while getting shot at themselves. "What better birthday present could I have asked for than to take out those miserable Japs."

The Oregonian, from an interview with Nimitz, highlighted FLEET AIR WING FOUR's raids when U.S. naval forces started to gain a foothold in the northern Pacific:

"Paramushiro is 1200 miles north of Tokyo and has been the target of at least a dozen punishing air attacks since American re-conquest of the western Aleutians last summer. The latest air blow was struck the night of the naval bombardment with Aleutians based bombers hammering Paramushiro and Shumshu, from a tiny outpost. The naval attack by a task force of undisclosed strength was aimed at the south and east coast of Paramushiro, sites of strategic shore installations previously mapped by the air raiders. The planes of Commodore Leslie Gehres' Fleet Air-Wing Four were back last night, the second consecutive night of their resumed 'Empire Express.' They hit shortly after the naval bombardment."

FLEET AIR WING FOUR was very successful with their Aleutian operations and the public were now becoming more knowledgeable of the successes. And Doris and the family were now aware of what Jack had been doing for his country.

THE SECRETARY OF THE NAVY
WASHINGTON

The President of the United States takes pleasure in presenting the AIR MEDAL to

LIEUTENANT, JUNIOR GRADE, JACK RICHARD INGRAM
UNITED STATES NAVY

for service as set forth in the following

CITATION:

"For meritorious achievement in aerial flight as a Technical Observer (Aerologist), attached to Fleet Air Wing FOUR, and operating with Patrol Bombing Squadron ONE HUNDRED THIRTY NINE, ONE HUNDRED THIRTY SIX and ONE HUNDRED THIRTY FIVE, during operations against enemy Japanese forces in the Aleutian and Kurile Islands Areas from March 6 to August 28, 1944. Completing his fifth mission during this period, Lieutenant, Junior Grade, (then Aerographer) Ingram provided expert analyses of weather conditions in the target area and thereby contributed materially to the success of our forces in the area. His courage and devotion to duty in the face of grave hazards were in keeping with the highest traditions of the United States Naval Service."

For the President,

Secretary of the Navy

Air Medal Citation

Admiral Nimitz commended FLEET AIR WING FOUR for the success of their missions: "17 May, 1944 – To the personnel of Fleet Air-Wing Four whose high morale and aggressive operations under trying weather conditions command my respect and admiration! With best wishes, C. W. Nimitz"

Nimitz also recommended Jack for the Navy Air Medal for the missions he flew during air reconnaissance and bombing. The Navy Air Medal is awarded "to anyone while serving in any capacity in or with the Armed Forces of the United States who distinguishes himself or herself by meritorious achievement while participating in aerial flight."

Jack's personal citation read,

"For meritorious achievement in aerial flight as a Technical Observer (Aerologist) attached to Fleet Air-Wing Four and operating with PATROL BOMBING SQUADRON ONE HUNDRED THIRTY-NINE AND ONE HUNDRED THIRTY-SIX AND ONE HUNDRED THIRTY-FIVE, during operations against enemy Japanese forces in the Aleutian and Kurile Island Area from March 6 to August 28, 1944. Completing his fifth mission during this period, Lieutenant, Junior Grade (then Warrant Officer and Chief Aerologist) Ingram provided expert analyses of weather conditions in the target area and thereby contributed materially to the success of our forces in the area. His courage and devotion to duty in the face of grave hazards were in keeping with the highest traditions of the United Sates Naval Services.

"For the President

"John L Sullivan, Secretary of the navy"

Such a commendation from the "old man" was truly appreciated by Jack! He also got a signed photograph from Admiral Nimitz, which he treasured.

During this time, while Jack was away from home, Doris gave birth to Beverly Louise 7 lb., 2 oz, on April 25, 1944, in Portland, Oregon. This was hard for Jack because he knew that he would not have the opportunity to see Bev for perhaps a year or more.

By this time, Jack Ingram was the only aerographer who had flown missions with all three of the squadrons listed in the citation: the 135th,

Weather station and office on Attu

the 136th, and the 139th Patrol Bombing Squadrons operating with FLEET AIR WING FOUR in the Aleutians during World War II.

Several of Jack's tougher missions were fraught with danger. From Attu Island, from June to September 1944, Jack would fly on weather and bombing missions to Japanese-held Kurile Island of Paramushiro, as well as to Onekotan Kaikye, Ichinowntari Wan, Shimushu, Shirinski, Kurabu Zaki, Kashimabara, and Kamchatka in the Aleutians.

Naval air operations in the Aleutians were quite different from air operations in the European theater. Men of the Eighth Air Force in Europe charged with the destruction of the Nazi empire had to fly twenty-five missions for their tour of duty. Then they would return to the States. Con-

Personal photo and note given to Jack from Nimitz

sidering the German Luftwaffe and the anti-aircraft defense of Europe, it is no wonder that the Eighth Air Force alone lost more than 50,000 airmen in their mission of gaining air superiority over the German Luftwaffe.

Artist proof of WWII "Empire Night Express" art work for a plane

In contrast, the Aleutian raids were quite different. To have flown more than eighty missions as Jack Ingram did, considering the weather, he wondered which duty was worse. The ground crews had to repair aircraft and get them ready for morning flights. Their only protection was a canvas windshield and maybe a barrel of kerosene set afire. Their hands were covered in clumsy, fur-lined, deerskin mittens, and they had to handle tools and perform intricate work on aircrafts' engines. And yet, day after day, night after night, they persevered.

Jack continued to inspire the pilots and to give them the most accurate weather forecasts possible—to keep them flying. Lieutenant Commander R. H. Maynard and Commodore L. E. Gehres (FLEET AIR WING FOUR Commander) recommended Jack for a commission and he was appointed ensign, U.S. Navy, on December 15, 1944.

Due to the nature of the low-level air attacks in the Aleutians, a problem arose. The bombing missions were having difficulty with the attacking aircraft getting caught in bomb blasts. One PV-1 attacked so low they were caught in their own and other plane's bomb blasts. The pilot literally "shot himself down" this way and was forced to land his crippled plane on Kamchatka. Another PV-1 returned to Attu with a gaping hole in one wing in which was lodged a large chunk of Japanese sod. Eventually, a solution was found. Delayed fuses were employed on bombs as a safeguard for future low-flying missions.

After every mission weather briefing, Jack would exclaim, "Let's go fly the weather!" The daylight Empire Express intruder attacks soon became search-and-destroy missions. Targets included not only enemy airfields, parked planes, and related installations, but also coastal freighters, tankers, fishing boats, canneries, docks, warehouses, radar stations, and radio stations up and down the coasts of Shimushu and Paramushiro. Marauding sweeps were also made into the Sea of Okhotsk in search of shipping. Missions were usually carried out by PV-1's flying cloaked in fog or low clouds—guided by flying aerologists using the weather as an advantage.

Along with other aviation improvements, a top-secret new technological modification came to FLEET AIR WING FOUR in 1944. Secret LORAN VHF radios were installed into all PBY and PV-1 aircraft, allowing for sophisticated radio direction finders and VHF radios with radio altimeters. All navy planes were also fitted with improved high-altitude oxygen systems. New navy navigators brought the technology with them upon their arrival to Attu. LORAN was a system of long-range navigation in which pulsed signals sent out by two pairs of radio stations were used to determine geographical position. Both ground waves and sky waves could be used to provide coverage over an extensive area with few stations. One of the best features was that planes and ships could use LORAN without breaking radio silence.

Before LORAN, air operations were often carried out without benefit of sophisticated instrument landing approach systems, although rather primitive radio range stations were in operation. Signals from these were often obliterated by static. Putting this in perspective, when the Japanese bombed Pearl Harbor it had been only fourteen years since Charles A. Lindberg's historic Atlantic flight. It was a miracle that so many early navy air wing missions were completed safely!

In the Aleutians, the U.S. Navy weathermen took part in one of the strangest campaigns ever fought. Actions took place along a chain of scattered islands, steaming volcanoes, snowcapped peaks, innumerable

Jack's Fleet Air Wing Four bomber jacket with Aleutian WWII patch

Attu air strip

fjords, and torturously jagged terrain that stretched a thousand miles across oceans that are among the world's roughest. The campaign was fought in a savage clime and often under impossible conditions.

One of the most dreaded daily features of PV-1 weather missions to the Kuriles was the creeping and intense cold. Temperature decreases about 5 degrees with each 1,000 feet of altitude. It was not unusual for the aerographer's mate to record outside air temperatures of 50–70F below zero.

In total, Jack spent a month, from November to December, on Adak Island in 1943 as a warrant officer and chief aerographer, and a year on Attu from February 1944 to February 1945 forecasting and leading and flying missions for FLEET AIR WING FOUR. During Jack's Aleutian wartime duty, he would advance three ranks in the navy.

Perhaps one of the highest tributes paid to U.S. Aleutian airmen came from the enemy. Commander Shigefuso Hashimoto, of the Imperial Japanese Navy attached to Japanese Naval Headquarters at Tokyo, was interrogated after the war by Captain James S. Russell, an active duty U.S. Navy officer. In reference to the Aleutians, Commander Hashimoto stated that he, "Respected greatly that Americans flew and attacked in weather which the Japanese considered impossible for air operations." This was indeed high praise, considering it came from a member of a people that place such great value on courage.

Jack Ingram was one aerologist officer who instilled confidence and courage to help keep everyone in the best mental state to "fly the weather," which, incidentally, was Ingram's own personal quote. It became a battle cry for the Aleutian airmen.

Jack's seventh great leadership character trait was *confidence*!

Chapter Eight

The Honorable Maverick

The year 1944 went out with a roar when a typhoon struck Philippine waters on December 18. Admiral Halsey's senior staff aerologists, including Jack Ingram from the Aleutians, recommended a course change but Halsey chose to take Carrier Task Force 38 of his U.S. Third Fleet into the teeth of the typhoon. Three U.S. destroyers capsized and sank. Seven other ships were heavily damaged. Eight hundred officers and men lost their lives. One hundred eighty-six carrier planes broke their lashings and were blown over the side or were so badly damaged they had to be jettisoned.

In Halsey's fervor to catch the Japanese fleet, he abandoned all reasonable advice and tried to drive his task force through the center of the typhoon. Many navy officers and enlisted personnel respected his decision because they would follow him anywhere; others thought he was foolish. Jack thought Halsey to be unreasonable in this situation, but he also honored and respected the admiral for many other decisions he had made to help win the war. Conflicted, Jack decided to step back and think about the situation and ask himself what he could do to help the navy better understand typhoons, and how captains should navigate around storms in the future.

Admiral Nimitz appointed a board of inquiry presided over by Vice Admiral John H. Hoover. Admiral Hoover recommended that Admiral Halsey be court-martialed. However, Admiral Ernest J. King of the Joint Chiefs of Staff concurred with Admiral Nimitz that Halsey was too popular a figure with the public and with his men to be publicly censured because it would be too damaging for morale.

Nimitz issued a directive for dealing with typhoons and other severe storms to be authored by Father Deppermann, Commander Wilbur Lockhart, and Jack Ingram. Deppermann and Lockhart were the navy's foremost weather authorities and Jack's best mentors.

Despite his close call with court-martial and the Nimitz directive, Admiral Halsey took his carrier task force into the teeth of yet another typhoon on June 5, 1945. This time, the cruiser USS *Pittsburgh* lost her bow, 32 other ships were damaged, and 142 aircraft were destroyed. Once again, Hoover was appointed to head a board of inquiry. Again, the board placed most of the blame on Halsey. As many guessed would happen, Halsey received only a reprimand, but not listening to timely aerographer forecasts to avoid the second typhoon almost cost him his career.

Jack felt that Halsey never took their weather reports and briefings seriously, whereas Nimitz considered them vital to operations. Jack wasn't sure whether the issue was a lack of trust in the newly developed science of aerology, or whether Halsey's pursuit of victory and glory was blinding him.

After the second typhoon catastrophe, Jack respectfully recommended to Commander Lockhart and Admiral Nimitz that the navy track, research, and document all the typhoons in the western Pacific from August through October 1945.

Jack was now a navy officer. Without finishing high school, he was a true "Navy maverick"—a man who rose through the ranks from an enlisted man to an officer. He was well respected and his colleagues and commanding officers were listening.

By now the winds of war were abating and in May 1945 the world saw the defeat of the Nazi empire in Europe. Resisting all attempts at a negotiated peace, the Allies demanded and received an "unconditional surrender."

In July of 1945, a month before Japan's ultimate defeat, Jack was recognized for his intelligence and aptitude by being ordered by Commander Lockhart to Fleet Weather Central at Pearl Harbor. He was the Pacific fleet liaison for forecasting daily weather reports with the help of twenty navy aerographers who reported to him. Later, Lockhart sent orders for Jack to attend the new, famed meteorology and oceanography course at the Scripps Institution of Oceanography in California. Jack could hardly believe it; he was going home to Doris!

Scripps Institution of Oceanography (Jack is in the front row – third from left)

It would be the first time Jack would see his second daughter, Beverly Louise Ingram. Bev was one-and-a-half years old and did not know her daddy when he came to the door. The war had kept him away for too long!

Scripps was an excellent career advancement opportunity because the course was run by the University of California at San Diego. The Scripps Institution was becoming one of the most important centers of ocean, Earth, and atmospheric science, research, education, and public service in the world. Men selected for this training were among the best of the best in U.S. Navy aerology. It was the Top Gun of navy aerological science and a feather in the cap of any navy aerologist.

Jack's studies at Scripps encompassed physical, chemical, biological, geological, and geophysics studies of the ocean, Earth, and planets. Scripps' transformative research opportunities in ocean and climate science and policy helped Jack to better understand the collective forces of the Earth.

While at Scripps, Jack had intensive training in the natural forces that affect high-altitude balloon flight. Balloon research and development was part of his lighter-than-air curriculum at Scripps, helping to further define Jack's meteorology education. It helped him to understand how to forecast upper stratosphere dynamics for future top-secret air force and navy CIA/NSA spy balloon deployment and reconnaissance missions.

After completing his studies at the Scripps Institution, Jack was ordered to the COM SEVENTH AMPHIB FORCE. In August 1945 Jack wrote, with a gusto the whole nation shared, "World War II ends—on my way west again (western Pacific), aboard the USS *Catoctin*."

Jack's skills continued to develop along with advancements in technology. Although he remained frustrated that Halsey never listened to his and other aerologists' forecasts and typhoon warnings, Jack decided to maintain respect, stay positive, and develop another way to communicate by writing a book about typhoons—so that Halsey and every other navy commanding officer could make better future decisions on how to avoid them.

Jack's eighth great leadership character trait was *respect*!

Chapter Nine
Aerology and Intelligence

USS *Catoctin* was an Appalachian class amphibious force flagship; in other words, a communication, intelligence, and headquarters ship. Jack was the ship's aerology officer and assistant intelligence officer in charge of six aerologists and ten intelligence personnel with the COM SEVENTH AMPHIB FORCE, serving on the staff of Vice Admiral Daniel Barbey. Barbey knew of Jack's leadership attributes and high-level communication skills while serving in the Aleutians. He quickly became Jack's first influential navy intelligence mentor. Underway at sea, Jack wrote a publication called, "Sea Surface Indications of Wind Velocity" that the navy sent to captains throughout the Pacific fleet. The document helped captains and crew to better understand the influences of wind on ship speed for operations, especially for aircraft carrier operations.

Interestingly, Vice Admiral Barbey grew up in Portland, Multnomah County, Oregon; thus, Jack and the admiral had a lot in common. Jack made friends easily and he always valued his friendships at the highest levels. He often advised others, "You'll have very few good friends in life and when you find one—honor and value him forever!"

In early September, Jack was personally selected to be part of Vice Admiral Barbey's staff for the Japanese surrender on board USS *Missouri* in Tokyo Bay. It was a momentous occasion and the ship was packed with American sailors and foreign nationals from all the allied nations. It was a great honor to be selected for this extraordinary occasion. After the ceremony, Jack had a chance to say hello to Admiral Nimitz, whom he personally knew from many years forecasting. Admiral Halsey was also present, and Jack overheard him telling Barbey, "Good luck with our other surrender ceremonies this month and, if you see any Japs flying around, politely shoot them down!"

While the most famous image of the Japanese surrender was aboard USS *Missouri* in Tokyo Bay, other ceremonies marked the Japanese ouster from the Japanese mainland to the Korean peninsula. In his laconic and modest way, Jack made terse mention of some of these history-making occasions that he helped to oversee and document for the United States. In September and October 1945, he wrote, "Visited in order: Tientsin, Chinwangtao, Weihaiwei, Hulu-tao, Yinkou, and Shanghai, China."

On Sept. 9 Jack found himself present with Vice Admiral Barbey's staff for the Japanese surrender of Korea in Seoul. The young man who joined the navy for adventure was taking part in one of history's most memorable events.

Later that month, on September 25, Jack was part of a mission to embark marines for duty in China to help oversee negotiations between Chinese nationalists and Chinese communists. This was a tense situation. With the abrupt end to the war, the Japanese defeat and collapse allowed the communists to gain control in the Northern provinces. Chiang Kai-shek and Mao Zedong negotiated, but they got nowhere. By the end of October, heavy fighting broke out over Manchuria following the Soviet departure.

While in China, Jack came to some sobering conclusions. Being in the navy was not just a youthful adventure. He was part of a military organization whose job, duty, and obligation was to protect the United States, including fighting wars with enemies. He saw the terrible evidence of the aftermath of war in the Japanese atrocities committed against the Chinese people, which included unspeakable barbarism such as decapitating people just to show off the sharpness and accuracy of their Samurai swords. Jack, and all Americans, were appalled by such ugly and gruesome acts.

Jack was haunted by the brutal images of dozens of severed Chinese heads laying in rice paddies throughout the region. While he traveled the countryside, Jack was glad that his Colt .45 pistol was snug on his hip. In fact, he carried an extra-long clip just in case he ran into any Japanese soldiers carrying swords. He was alert for snipers in trees along the dirt roads. There were occasional reports of Japanese soldiers remaining after the war, likely not even aware the war was over. One time, Jack picked up a long Japanese sniper rifle, though he didn't record the story behind it in his journal.

Horrific photo taken from a Japanese officer's pocket during surrender

While on the *Catoctin*, Jack served well as the aerology officer and excelled as an assistant intelligence officer. Though he was not specifically trained in navy intelligence, it was the navy's practice to handpick smart, skilled, competent men for intelligence work that they were deemed suited for, especially if they had experience intercepting Japanese wartime code, proving their aptitude for such classified assignments.

No playbook existed for post–WWII navy intelligence, and Jack participated in creating the protocols and discipline for intelligence work in the navy. On a ship like USS *Catoctin*, a control and command vessel, early naval intelligence was a bit more than routine. President Truman was very interested in the intelligence that Admiral Barbey and *Catoctin's* team collected while on their mission to oversee Japanese surrenders, negotiations, and interrogation throughout the Pacific.

Overseeing the signing of surrender papers and politely interrogating Japanese officers and soldiers became routine for Barbey and his delegation of navy and marine officers, including Jack Ingram. With the help of a translator, Jack was especially adept at asking Japanese detainees, "Can you please tell me . . . ?" Japanese officers learned to be honest with Jack and others because Barbey's interrogation team would treat cooperating surrendering Japanese with dignity while keeping suspicious, dissenting, or uncooperative Japanese soldiers in a holding area for future long-term interrogation.

Moreover, Barbey was given strict orders to arrest Japanese officers and soldiers who had played a role in any war atrocities. Barbey's team had a short watchlist of these war criminals from actual photos taken and kept by surrendering Japanese of their soldiers decapitating Chinese and American prisoners. Identifying such Japanese criminals from intelligence gathered and collected from returning U.S. prisoners of war (POWs) and Japanese soldiers themselves was not difficult.

During this time, Jack wrote classified briefs for Barbey that were sent to the Pentagon and used to communicate their observations and activities in the Pacific. His clear and concise, "no bullshit" briefs were welcomed by U.S. intelligence agencies.

Jack coached his navy intelligence advance collection team on how to acquire information from surrendering Japanese officers and other local sources. Jack had a gift for finding out what Japanese officers really wanted and needed. Jack told his men, "Jap officers just want freedom and a chance to go home, so getting information from them is easy." With the help of U.S. Marines, detaining Japanese officers was common practice before, during, and in some cases, after formal surrender ceremonies had taken place. Japanese officers were detained to verify intelligence information. In some cases, Japanese officers would try to impersonate lower-ranking soldiers so they could be released earlier, but they never fooled Barbey's team.

Aside from intelligence, while on the *Catoctin* another of Jack's aerology missions was his completion of *Typhoons of the Western Pacific.* The book was applauded by numerous Pacific navy captains. Well received by Barbey, Nimitz, Halsey, and many other admirals, the publication became required reading by all Pacific navy captains. It was the first of its kind for the navy! For Jack, unlike so many other responsibilities, it was something he could talk about.

Japanese rifle taken off a sniper

By maintaining profound respect for Halsey, and by compartmentalizing incomprehensible WWII operational fleet decisions made by him, Jack was able to constructively influence future commanding officer decision-making regarding typhoons and other catastrophic storms like hurricanes.

Jack learned one of life's important lessons during this period of his life. He later advised, "You can't do anything about poor decisions others make, but you can come to understand why they made them and never do the same thing yourself." He also said, "You always have the opportunity to show people the facts that can help them make better decisions." He garnered such simple philosophy from his time interacting with Halsey, when he turned a negative catastrophic situation into something positive for the future. *Typhoons of the Western Pacific* highlighted Jack as a man that commanding officers would see as someone the navy should commit to at a higher level.

Jack completed *Typhoons of the Western Pacific* in an advancing technological time when the navy sought people who could think about ways to analyze fundamental questions and answer complex problems.

Jack never forgot about his intelligence and aerology teams that helped to support vital U.S. naval duties. He wrote the following in the preface: "This brief study is the result of the efforts of the following men. Without their wholehearted cooperation and extra hours of work it could not have been produced." Even though he could not speak about his intelligence team, he could mention many of the same men in the realm of aerology. Key personnel of Seventh Amphibious Force Aerological Unit:

Typhoons of the Western Pacific authored by Jack

White, Benjamin U. AerM 1/c USNR
Lauver, Clifford P. AerM 1/c USNR
Ulrich, J. C. AerM 2/c USNR
Darnell, R J. AerM 3/c
Iacono, J. V. AerM 3/c USNR
Barker, W H. Rdm 2/c USNR

Commander Dimitrijevic on the *Catoctin* acknowledged Jack in the following way:

"Ensign J. R. Ingram, U.S.N. who deserves special mention for the neat and skillful manner in which he redrew the maps reproduced herein from his original analyses, and for his general supervision of the entire project. To him is due the credit for the labor in preparing the framework upon which this book is based. The officers and men of the photographic unit of the U.S.S. *Catoctin* who produced the books. To all the foregoing my thanks and deep appreciation.

"W. J. Dimitrijevic, Commander, U.S. Navy."

Later, Chief of Naval Operations and Admiral Daniel E. Barbey, Commander, Amphibious Forces, who was now assigned to the Atlantic fleet, requested copies of Jack's new book in the following way:

"It is requested that as many copies as are available up to the number 100 of reference is furnished. Aerology, Flight Section, Office of the Chief of Naval Operations for further distribution to the naval services. This excellent study of tropical cyclones (typhoons) was prepared on board the U.S.S. *Catoctin* by the Aerological Unit of Commander Seventh Amphibious Force. As an important contribution to amphibious operations, it deserves further disseminations."

The book was to be given to navy captains of the Atlantic fleet to better understand the habits of Northern Hemisphere hurricanes. During this time, Admiral Barbey wrote the following note to Jack:

"This weather research study *Typhoons of the Western Pacific August to October of 1945*, produced by the Aerological Unit of Commander Seventh Amphibious forces, constitutes an important contribution to amphibious operations and requests additional copies for further distribution to the naval service Commander Amphibious Forces, Atlantic, as former Commander Seventh Amphibious forces knows that your technical ability and extra hours of effort contributed materially to the production of this study. He takes pleasure, therefore, in commending you for the initiative and professional ability you have displayed—A copy of this letter will be entered in your next fitness report."

Jack clearly understood how important an officer's fitness report is to his career and advancement and, with a growing family, Jack certainly could use the promotion. He truly had a good friend in Admiral Barbey and he appreciated this friendship and others during those postwar days.

Jack's ninth great leadership character trait was *his ability to honor friendship*!

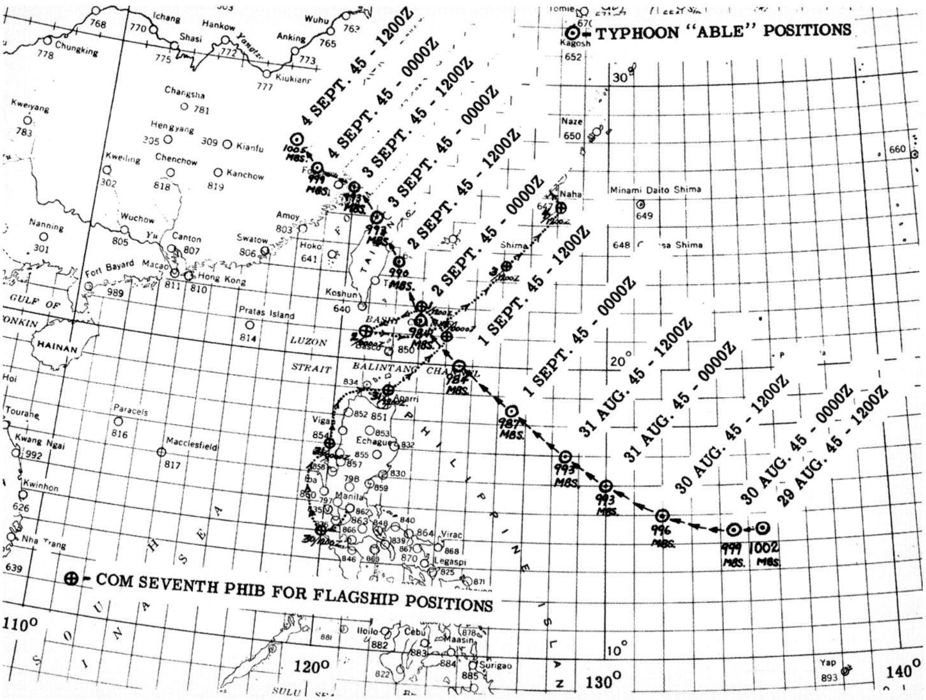

A selection of Maps drawn by Jack Ingram for the U.S. Navy publication, *A Study of Six Typhoons of the Western Pacific*

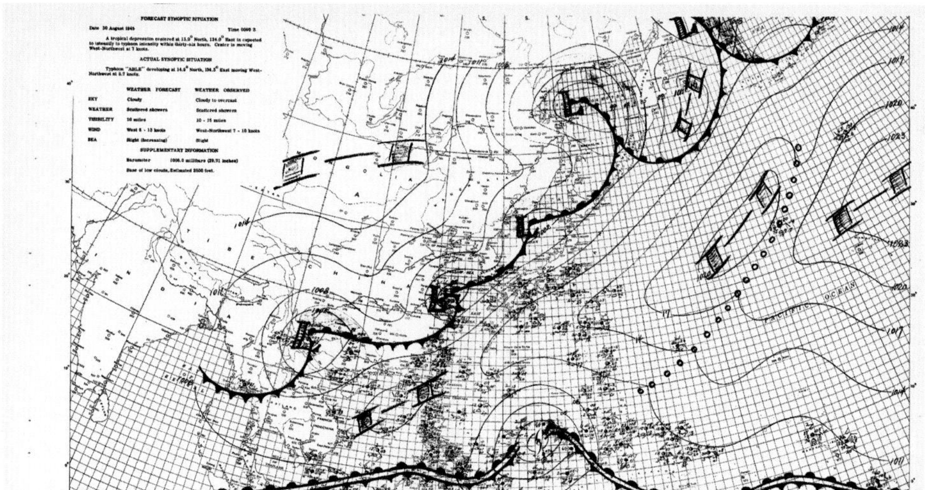

Chapter Ten

Naval Justice

The war was over, and, for the men of the regular navy, peacetime duty was both promising and yet bound to be slow in the way of promotions. It was a time when most regular army and navy men had to consider if they would continue in their careers as professional military men. Jack struggled to decide what to do, but Doris told him that she'd support whatever decision he made. Ultimately, with his growing family and the need for a more permanent and higher pay rating, Jack stuck with the navy. He was intent on climbing the ranks as high as possible. It was truly a time that weeded out the professional military men from the masses of brave soldiers and sailors who helped win the war.

At this point in his life, Jack looked within himself and thought about his past and what he had achieved, where he was in the present, and the opportunities in the future if he continued to apply himself. Echoing in his mind was the advice his father had once given to him, "Work hard and always do the right thing!"

From March 1946 through April of 1947, Jack was assigned to COM GULF SEA FRONTIER, stationed in Norfolk, Virginia, in charge of forty-five navy aerographers and intelligence personnel. Once again, Jack's duties were split. He was both advising the Atlantic fleet and working with the Pentagon on daily weather reports, including hurricane warnings and navy intelligence matters throughout the Atlantic. All this time, he was being groomed for future high-level intelligence missions.

Not long after, Jack was stricken with grief once again. In a journal entry from October 16, 1946, he wrote, "Earl Burns Ingram, my father, age 64 died suddenly in his sleep. During his life, he had been a farmer, cowboy, railroad man, logger, ship builder, boilermaker, contractor, union secretary, and a fine 'Daddy.' He was a former president of L-72 Boilermaker AFL Union. He constructed the KOIN radio towers of Portland, Oregon, the first freshwater pipelines of Dalles, Oregon, and the Oak Grove pipelines of Portland. He was buried in Rose City, Portland, Oregon."

Earl had been born in Bowie, Texas, in 1882. Bowie, a town of less than five hundred souls, had little to offer. Its main claim to fame was that it was named after the hero of the Alamo and inventor of the famous Bowie knife, Jim Bowie. Bowie was a significant staging area for the railway to the West—rail that Earl traveled out of town on to Colorado when he left home in 1896. He then purchased a horse and rode it over the Rocky Mountains, eventually settling in Oregon. Earl had little chance to make a living in Bowie unless he wanted to be a cowboy or continue working on the rail line, and there was no money in either of those endeavors.

Earl's brother, Jack's Uncle Bill, had left the farm to become the first schoolteacher for the Kickapoo Indians, and his parents had sold the farm. Bowie was not much of a place for a young man to start off in life without any resources or family support. So Earl worked his way northwest to Portland, Oregon, and eventually learned to be a steel worker, a pipefitter, and then a boilermaker.

Jack's rather perfunctory eulogy no doubt masked the deep pain that he felt as he remembered his dad and their amazing adventures on the Rogue River, something few other fathers and sons were able to experience.

From April to May 1947, while being attached to COM GULF SEA FRONTIER, Jack served on special assignment aboard the aircraft carrier USS *Sicily*, where he was the chief aerologist and chief intelligence officer in charge of eight personnel. Soon afterward, he was asked to attend the Naval School of Justice.

Jack reported to Naval Justice School on December 19, 1947. This was a ten-week course at Naval Station Newport in Rhode Island. The mission of the school was to instruct navy, marine corps, and coast guard enlisted men and officers in the fundamental principles of military justice, as well as civil and administrative law procedures. The training was to enable the graduates to deliver quality legal service and to promote justice and sea service fleet readiness.

Jack's excellent communication skills were a good fit for military justice considering his aptitude for assimilating information and writing clear, effective briefs. This training could have been the start of a career-changing course, but Jack wanted to broaden his horizons by building on what he had, to find more opportunities in the peacetime navy and support his growing family.

Jack had now achieved his cherished dream to be promoted to the officer ranks as a lieutenant junior grade, and his commanding officer asked him to join VPM 3, the Hurricane Hunter Squadron in Miami, Florida. The name later changed to VPHL-3, which was designated as a Heavy Patrol Squadron. There Jack was designated Naval Aviation Observer (NAO)—Aerology. His unique WWII experiences "flying the weather" in the Aleutians made him a logical choice for this duty.

Jack was able to spend Christmas and New Year at home with his family in Miami that year, a rare treat. There was no happier time for Jack than being home with his family for the holidays. "Home is the sailor, home from the sea!"

But it wasn't long before Jack moved his family to Atlantic City, New Jersey, for a new, short intelligence mission assignment. While there he flew intelligence missions to Argentina and Newfoundland that remain classified. After this short stint in Atlantic City, Jack found himself packing up Doris, Karen, and Beverly and moving back to Miami. The life of a military family often involves many moves, but Jack's family moved more than most. They liked Miami, though, and were happy to return.

With the new job, however, Jack, Doris, and the kids were about to embark on an adventure in the navy together. Maybe the navy, in its wisdom, realized that as a man matures he is bound to want to be with his family more and see his children grow up.

Jack's latest assignment allowed him to advance his career without sacrificing invaluable time with his young family. Now that he had this opportunity he spent more time thinking about his experiences and how he could pass on what he had learned to his children.

Jack's tenth great leadership character trait was *introspection*!

Hurricane captured on early RADAR

Chapter Eleven

From Typhoons to Hurricanes

In the 1940s the dangerous practice of hurricane hunting with aircraft was in its infancy. It actually started as a dare when, in July 1943, Lieutenant Colonel Joseph Duckworth of the Army Air Force took an AT-6 single-engine training plane and flew the flimsy craft into the eye of a hurricane in Texas.

The Joint Hurricane Warning Center (JHWC) had been established on July 14, 1943, when the Weather Bureau's Hurricane Warning Service office was transferred from Jacksonville, Florida, to Miami and located with the Army Air Force's Hurricane Office and the navy's Miami-based Navy Weather Central. The navy base was located just northeast of Miami in Opa-locka, and that was where Jack, Doris, Karen, and Beverly lived.

Navy hurricane reconnaissance flights began that same year. Several initial flights were flown into tropical storms in July and August out of San Juan, Puerto Rico, with Navy PBY Catalina and PBM Mariner flying boats from FLEET AIR WING 11. The first *authorized* flight into an Atlantic hurricane occurred in September 1943 when a Navy PBY from San Juan penetrated an unnamed hurricane 250 miles from Puerto Rico. The aircraft skirted the inner edge of the storm's eye for more than five hours at 550 feet.

When Jack joined the group in 1948, he worked with the meteorological squadron of the Atlantic command. This squadron contributed to the research and development of the now-famous technique of low-level penetration of the hurricane eye (100 feet off the water). Flying low into hurricanes by dodging large waves took tremendous courage and skill. Jack flew hurricane reconnaissance flights to locate, track, and provide storm information crucial for the U.S. Weather Bureau to issue warnings and forecasts to cities such as Miami. Of course, Miami was in the heart of the "hurricane belt."

In May 1948, the *Oregon Journal* interviewed Jack while he was on leave from the "hurricane belt" visiting family in Oregon.

"Ingram doesn't talk much about the danger but makes it obvious that flying into a cyclonic wind blowing at a velocity of 60 knots on the perimeter and up to 140 knots near the center is no picnic. He relates, 'Our object is to reach the eye of the hurricane,' Ingram said. 'That's a spot in the center which might be from 5 to 20 miles in diameter and where there is almost a dead calm. From there we can predict with considerable accuracy the direction and speed that the storm is moving. We transmit the information to the Navy Weather Central, which, in turn, broadcasts warnings to the areas in the United States where the hurricane is expected to strike. If from this information a city can avoid having to go "under wraps" for a storm which won't hit, it can save itself millions of dollars. If on the other hand a city knows it is going to be hit it can batten down the hatches and such relief units such as the Red Cross and National Guard could be mobilized.'

"For this work the navy uses Privateer Aircraft, big, rugged, four-engine planes. The Privateer was similar to the Army's Liberator but the fuselage was longer in order to accommodate a flight engineer's station. It had a tall, single, vertical stabilizer rather than the twin boom tail configuration.

"One went down in a Category One typhoon near Bataan Island in the Philippines. It crash-landed on the island, and none of the six hurricane hunters were lost.

"Other than that, there was only one other fatality among the hunters.

"'Normally we fly at an altitude of 500 feet,' Ingram said. 'The winds are accompanied by torrential rains which infiltrate everything in the ship. Visibility is nil and usually we are able to determine our altitude only by our radar altimeter. It's like flying an airplane in a giant washing machine.'

"The reason for choosing the low altitude is that vertical drafts are at a minimum. From the highest altitudes, the plane might be dropped a thousand feet at a bounce.

"Ingram was glad his plane had 8,000 feet of altitude on one occasion when all four engines conked out at once from oxygen deficiency in the rain laden air, something that could never happen to an aircraft in flight unless you were part of that dauntless band of Hurricane Hunters.

VPM 3 – Hurricane Hunter Squadron – Miami

"A Privateer had the gliding capacity of a railroad boxcar! It was a miracle that the pilot was able to restart the engines and get them going again. Needless to say, that was the happiest Navy crew ever!"

Another article in the *Miami Daily News* depicts a navy weather experiment.

"The navy made plans for a unique and controversial experiment to alter a storm, which, if successful, might change the name and designation of the Hurricane Hunters into 'Hurricane Wreckers.'

"The project included Jack Ingram and involved the bombing of cloud formations with carbon dioxide in solidified form to cause precipitation and prematurely release the vast store of potential destructive energy contained in the moisture of the clouds.

"In two weeks Navy Commander Edwin Harding, Commander of the hurricane weather central at Miami naval air station, said they would use the research of Professor Irving Langmuir, Nobel Prize winner, to bombard the cloud formations and change the nature of the hurricane. This was not an experiment that looked for a way to bust a storm but a way to dissipate it and make it less harmful.

"At that time, an Army B-29 manned by personnel of both Army and Navy services will seek a heavy cloud formation and will attack it from above, bombarding it with granules of dry ice. This is expected to create a snowstorm but, in this climate, it is not believed that the snow will last long enough to reach the earth.

"The hurricane is attacked at the snow level at an altitude high enough so that it is probable that snow will form. The precipitation would undoubtedly turn to raindrops long before it hit the sea or land.

"Hurricanes are great natural engines packed with energy. A fully developed one often measures 300 miles across the area of hurricane winds with an even larger area of storm and squalls extending in advance of the center. An unlimited supply of moist, hot air is required for them to develop. A paradox is this. Heat is required to transform liquid water into water vapor. This heat then becomes stored up in the moist air which a hurricane must have to live. But a hurricane precipitates vast quantity of rain, and in condensing water vapor into rain, the latent heat is released and adds its energy to the already unbelievable power of the storm. Weather experts believe

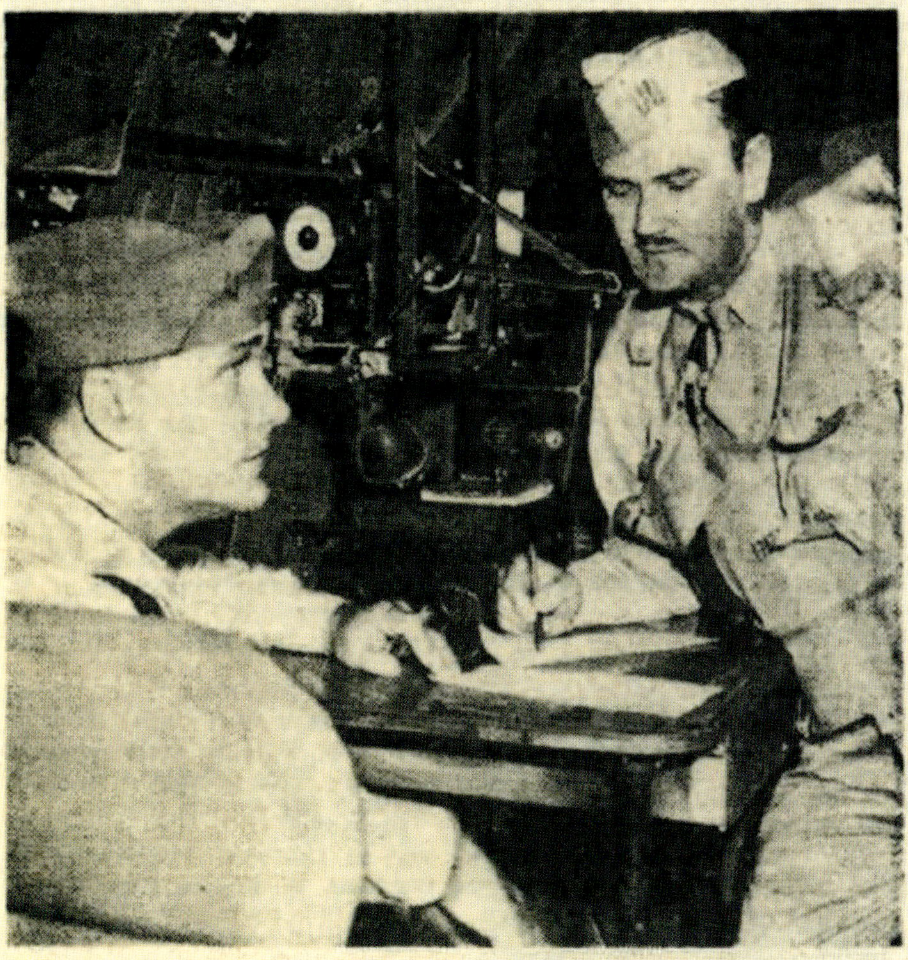

—Miami Daily News photo by Lucas

NAVY AND ARMY STORM OBSERVERS

Lt. (jg) Ingram (left) and Capt. Thompson

Jack discussing hurricane hunting on board a search plane

that this release of energy to condensation and precipitation is the secret of a continuing source of power which permits a great hurricane to travel as much as 2,000 miles and strike land with undiminished fury. At the time, this method was considered the most practical way to control a hurricane.

"On Saturday, Lt. Commander Collis O. Marshall, executive officer of VPHL-3, the navy's hurricane hunting squadron, and Navy Aerologist Jack R. Ingram flew the 2,500-mile track to San Juan in a B-17 Army aircraft, making the return trip in an Army B-29 the following day."

Unfortunately, the mission did not have the results hoped for. Mixing the carbon dioxide at high altitudes did not work! That said, missions like these helped scientists better understand the study and potential control of future hurricanes.

In another account, filed from Guantánamo Bay, Cuba, a newspaper reporter said, "I flew here from Florida over the largest and most dangerous hurricane in years. We were in a Navy PB4Y2, a four engine Privateer, over the roof of the mighty storm taking radar readings in its eye which is the calm center of a blowing hell.

"From 10,000 feet, it was a seething mixture of oil and milk in a witch's cauldron.

"Two hours after we left Miami, Lt. Jack Ingram, the aerographer aboard motioned me to a Plexiglas port in the side of the ship. 'That's it!' he yelled over the din of the engine.

"At about 6,500 feet menacing black clouds boiled and seethed like the dark smoke of a huge forest fire. Occasionally there was a break in the cloud mass and far below we could see the wind crazed ocean.

"The water was whipped into waves that leapt a hundred feet high and broke against the wind in a frothy mass. Ingram estimated that the wind was raging at 110 to 160 miles per hour according to the distance from the eye.

"It was all in miniature from our altitude. It looked like the whirlpool of the Niagara River seen from the small end of a telescope during a thunderstorm.

"The fury was unbelievable. We were still sailing along like a trip to dreamland on an innerspring mattress.

"We flew over to take a look at Great Abaco Island in the Bahamas about 200 miles off Miami. We dropped through the upper stratus of clouds and there the devastated island lay almost swept bare, with flattened palms pointing in the direction of the storm. Half gone.

"Etched in the shadow of the circular glass was the miniature of the worst tropical storm in years. Following Ingram's guidance, I found the becalmed eye lying like a corkscrew.

"We took another quick ride over the storm, ducked through a hole in the clouds that looked like a gaping hole in the roof of a circus tent, stared at the frothy ocean, and then beat it."

Much was learned from these navy missions. Sadly, there had previously been a lot of misinformation resulting in tragedy because of ignorance of hurricane development. An example is the case of the 1926 hurricane that struck Miami directly. Many lives had been lost and much property damage sustained through ignorance of the calm hurricane center and second half of the storm if it strikes directly. Because the wind movement is circular the first and second halves of storms that strike directly will blow from opposite directions.

Another account came from a colorful, well-known Miami radio reporter, Fred Olampitt, on July 18, 1947. Fred reported:

"On July 2 Commander Ted Harding appeared on The Rambler Program to tell WTOD listeners about hurricanes. But what I want to tell you this morning is the story of the men who fly through the hurricane, the men who hunt them down like some people go hunting rabbits or others go fishing.

"Somebody has to detect the first tropical disturbance... and that's my story. Just four weeks ago, I spent the weekend on a hunt for hurricanes. Through the courtesy of Lieutenant Commander William Jeneshek, Commanding Officer of VFM-3 and Commander Harding, I was able to make this two-day trip.

"A fortunate stroke of luck was to have a man like Navy Aerologist Lieutenant Jack Ingram to explain things to me.

"We flew in a PB4Y2 Privateer, a former bomber. It's a rugged thing, as it had to be, and, in some respect, it reminded me of a submarine with its narrow passages jam packed with gear and instrumentation.

"I was wearing a headset and could hear all the instructions that the skipper was giving to the crew. Sitting opposite in the co-pilot's seat was Ensign W. E Creel. Directly back of him, outside the cockpit is the aerologist's station with all its radar gadgets. Our aerologist was Lieutenant Ingram. Opposite, on the other side of the plane was Navigator Ensign H.N. (Bud) Ream. He's the man who tells you where you are and why. He also reports to the skipper the speed, advises on the course to pursue, and supplies the location to the radioman.

"The radioman, like everyone else aboard, never has a quiet moment. Location and weather reports are taken every half hour and sent back to the station hourly. Ingram, the aerologist, checks the wind and weather and his innumerable instruments, the wire recorder, the psychrometer, radio altimeter, pressure altimeter, 24-hour clock, aneroid barometer, and aerograph to mention a few. He seems to be busy constantly, his eyes and hands never still.

Director of *Slattery's Hurricane*

"There are eight men aboard these Navy weather planes. As I said before, all these men are volunteers, and all pretty brave men in my book. During the four-

Jack educating the public about hurricane hunting

month hurricane season these fellows may be here, there or anywhere. They stay in the designated spots of the Caribbean until they receive instructions to proceed to another. The men I flew with were family men. They sometimes don't see their families for weeks. When one is tracking a hurricane, he can't take time off to go home to the wife and kids.

"Listening through the headset of the intercom, one will hear an almost constant line of chatter between the pilot and the aerologist. This has a dual purpose. Most of the conversation is valuable, reports on the weather to the skipper and the radioman. The other purpose, by experienced men like Ingram, is to keep up the morale and spirit of the other men aboard.

"When a storm is reported it is charted. That's the interesting but dangerous task. Following previous reports, the great Navy plane is guided in the direction of the storm. Every man aboard has his eyes glued to his charts. The navigator gives the direction which the pilot follows ... into the unknown. The storm is sighted through the aerologist's instruments. There are times when the storm is so severe that the aerologist cannot write down all he sees through his instruments. When the plane is bouncing around in times like this he records the storm on a wire recorder for transmission later.

"But now they have found the storm. The problem is to get inside for the details awaited by their station back here in Miami and the Weather Bureau. Hurricanes swirl around counter-clockwise. And they swirl around at terrific speed. But the Navy plane has to get inside, into the eye. Although the eye might not be the center of the hurricane, its position has to be recorded to determine the course of the storm. And that, of course, is what it is all about, knowing where it is going to hit, so people can prepare.

"The eye of the storm is comparatively calm. But getting into it is the job. Since it turns counter-clockwise the Navy plane enters so the terrific winds hit the plane on the fuselage back of the left wing. The pilot doesn't waste any time getting inside. He holds the plane in a sharp turn. Despite his efforts to get there quickly, the plane and everyone aboard take some real cuffing and bouncing. Reaching the eye may take ten to sixty minutes battling hurricane winds of up to one hundred miles per hour. Can you imagine the tension during an hour of this? Can you imagine the average person's reaction to these conditions? No, of course not. No average person would ever do anything like this! Think about your last commercial airline flight and the heart thumping when the plane encountered some turbulence. Didn't you grab your partner's hand? Okay, I've made my point!

"And all this time while the pilot is fighting the plane and storm, the others aboard are busy at their work. Those rough minutes are what the weather stations want to know about. Why is it so important to get into the eye of the storm? Hurricanes, being more or less cylindrical-shaped things, the eye would naturally be the heart or center. Each report provides the position of the eye. In that way, the Weather Centrals can follow its direction. If it's headed for Miami, the first report has given a position for the eye, the wind velocity and intensity.

"This glimpse into a typical storm hunting mission gives one an example of what the courageous crew faces and goes through regularly during the hurricane season. Our hats off to these brave men."

Jack was not only courageous to go on these flights, he also kept talking to the pilot and crew, providing crucial information. His reassuring voice set the tone, keeping them calm and focused. He had gained a reputation for inspiring others to find courage beyond their normal boundaries, and Jack was called to action when inspiration was a necessity to complete missions.

Navy hurricane hunters also captured the imagination of the public when Jack was asked to be a navy technical advisor for the 1949 drama film *Slattery's Hurricane* starring Richard Widmark, Linda Darnell, and Veronica Lake. The filming took place in Miami. Jack, Doris, Karen, and Beverly even got to be extras in one of the scenes on the base.

Jack not only spent time with the cast and film crew, but he helped the actor Gary Merrill write the following narrative that's heard in the beginning of the film:

"This is a hurricane. Hurricanes are violent windstorms of great violence, several hundred miles in diameter, with a dead calm center called the eye. Like whirlpools, they spin rapidly, hurling great destruction in their paths. They're spawned in the doldrums, their father the heat of the sun, their mother the moisture of the sea. From July to December every year, the Caribbean crawls with these evil offspring of the elements."

The film project was fun and rewarding to work on. Jack and Doris were asked to spend a few nights out on the town with the actors.

Peacetime flying into hurricanes for the young, yet experienced, Lieutenant Jack Ingram was never scripted like a movie. It was just as

The Navy's hurricane hunting pilots

dangerous as his wartime missions. The big difference was he could return home from his missions into the loving arms of his family. Doris and their two little girls would often pick him up from the base after a mission. If there were photos to develop and reports to write, the debriefing would not be until the next day, and Jack could go straight home, still in his flight clothes.

For Jack, the ride home in the car was a chance to wind down from the built-up tension of the flight. One time, he was thinking about the brief he had to write the next morning and not paying much attention to the conversation in the car. Then, as he relaxed, he heard a small voice say, "I heard Mommy tell a lady that Daddy flew with a cane."

Little Beverly tapped her dad on the shoulder and asked, "Where's your cane, Daddy?"

Jack's attention perked up. He was trying to make sense of what he had just been asked. Bev's big sister, Karen, in a big-sister tone of voice, corrected, "She didn't say Daddy flew with a cane, silly. She said that Daddy flew into hurricanes." Jack and Doris exchanged a loving smile at their children's innocence, and for the pleasure of being together as a family.

R & R fishing the canals of Miami

Evenings meant home-cooked meals, fun with the family, and fishing for bass along the canals. Doris did everything she could to make a normal, happy family home. She handled the routine management of the household and children—as well as the occasional minor emergency—with calmness and efficiency. She was, after all, a navy wife!

And navy life wasn't easy. Each change of duty station involved moving household furnishings and changing schools for the kids. But Jack and Doris were a strong team and their marriage flourished!

Doris was a versatile woman. When she had her husband at home, her favorite thing to do was go dancing. Fortunately, unlike many husbands, Jack enjoyed this too—or, at least he went along with it. Doris also liked to go to church, to camp out, to explore, and to sing with her young family.

Jack was a good father and he spent time playing with his little daughters. But he was especially excited and grateful when, on March

2, 1949, they welcomed their first son, John Richard Ingram II, into the family. Jack could hardly believe it. He had a son.

Doris had to endure many separations from her husband, not only when he was at war, away at sea, but even during his shore duty. There was the added tension of the dangerous nature of his assignments and the risk of leaving the family fatherless in case of an accident. It was not easy for Doris when Jack explained his hurricane-hunting duties. But, as he told her, the navy had only one fatality among its hurricane hunters.

Jack exemplified courage in the war and in his duties as a hurricane hunter. But he also had the ability to instill and promote courage in others. He recognized that Doris, too, was courageous in her role as a navy wife and mother.

Jack's eleventh great leadership character trait was *courage*!

Chapter Twelve
A Higher Intelligence

By June 1949, Jack had completed duty as a hurricane hunter with Commander Harding in Miami and was ordered to the Staff COM PHIBGROUP TWO reporting to Rear Admiral Berk as staff aerologist, legal officer, and as a new intelligence officer.

For one year, Jack was now assigned off and on to USS *Mount Olympus*—flagship of the commander—Amphibious Group 2 out of Norfolk, Virginia, which was another headquarters and command vessel. It was headquarters for invasions and amphibious landings and was packed with navy intelligence and communications instruments. With twelve navy personnel under his command, Jack's duties consisted of the same split responsibilities as before, plus legal proceedings—forecasting for Atlantic amphibious force practice maneuvers along the Atlantic coast, overseeing all ship naval court proceedings, and interpreting and disseminating intelligence information gathered from all available sources.

As legal officer, Jack would oversee or serve on military panels of justice. He was known as a fair-minded officer who always recommended practical justice to help sailors in the long run, giving them every chance to correct their misguided ways and to step up and teach others to help shipmates who had the same propensity to get into trouble.

In 1950, the start of the Korean War, Jack received orders to report to the Office of Chief of Naval Operations, Navy Department, in Washington, D.C., which he did on May 30. His new job was administrative assistant for personnel to the Chief of Naval Operations, Pentagon.

Jack had proven himself to be an invaluable collector and disseminator of timely and accurate intelligence for the navy, and his superiors now wanted him to attend the new Naval Intelligence School. Jack finished at the top of his class with a 3.97 grade point average. The director of the Naval Intelligence School, Commander A. P. Slaff, stated in a

Relaxing with Doris

recommendation for Jack, "Jack Ingram has an excellent grasp of textual materials and he carefully studies the background and meaning of classified information before organizing his briefings. His content, organization, and quality of writing are of the highest caliber." After graduation, Jack was assigned as an instructor at the school because of his excellent communication skills, and he could teach others the same interactive techniques and applications. The Chief of Naval Operations also made Jack one of two dozen officers to be indoctrinated for the Armed Forces Security Agency (AFSA).

In 1947 the U.S. House of Representatives had held hearings to pass the navy Promotion Bill—H. R. 2537, refining a new category of navy officers known as the Limited Duty Officer (LDO). The navy drew up this new promotion bill because it recognized the reservoir of talented and valuable wartime temporary officers and prepared to make full use of their intellectual knowledge, skill, ambition, and loyalty. A navy LDO category would open the door for outstanding enlisted wartime temporary officers to advance to a permanent commission rank during peacetime. Jack was considered for the LDO category because of his outstanding record, years of service, leadership responsibilities, practical application experience, and skills.

In 1951, Jack was appointed to a permanent commission as a navy lieutenant in the Limited Duty Officer category. He noted in his journal, "My prayers have been heard!"

Doris having fun dancing on tables

While intelligence was becoming another one of his specialties, Jack did have real world experience during the war, and his commanding officers wanted the navy to benefit from his experiences, and, at the same time, broaden Jack's horizons. He had some of the highest recommendations as a young officer from his commanding officers. And his

Jack's 1953 military ID photo for NSA

duty was becoming anything but "limited!"

He did a fine job for the Chief of Naval Operations placing WWII veteran officers for duty around the world, while also excelling as a Naval Intelligence School instructor in Washington. During this time, the navy had indoctrinated him for AFSA responsibilities. AFSA was established within the U.S. Department of Defense under the command of the Joint Chiefs of Staff in Washington.

While in Washington, Jack had learned and then taught the art and science of cryptology, intercepting and deciphering the communications of foreign countries. Interestingly, Jack was taking courses in the German language, gearing up for a possible Cold War assignment. Battle tested from his past war assignments and studying, Jack burned the midnight oil every night.

Jack was ambitious, but he also knew that he had to do everything possible to obtain promotions to support his growing family. But advancement in the peacetime navy was tough. Not only was it slow, there just were not as many jobs as there had been in the wartime navy.

Jack had attended many service schools including aerology school at Lakehurst, Naval Justice School, Naval Intelligence School, as well as several civilian schools including the prestigious Scripps Institution at the University of California. He had earned his high school diploma from his old high school, Commerce High, while at sea. Later, he went on to college at the University of Oregon, the University of California, the University of Heidelberg, the University of Maryland, and the College of William and Mary. Jack understood the importance of a quality education.

While Jack was stationed in Virginia, he and Doris bought a beautiful little rambler house in McLean. They paid $18,400, and they had a mortgage of $15,900 plus another 4% under a GI Bill loan. McLean was considered way out in the country by Jack's pentagon friends, but Jack and Doris loved it. The local hardware in town became a great place to meet neighbors on Saturday mornings. A new Catholic church and school, St. John's, was being built less than a quarter mile away. For folks with roots in the Pacific Northwest, and as devout Catholics, Jack, Doris, and the family felt right at home.

The home in McLean was the first the Ingrams owned. It suggested a sense of permanency, or at least a place Jack could settle into where there would be no more uprooting of the family. Months later, Jack recorded in his journal, "A lot has happened since we bought our first and, perhaps, last house. On 11 January 1952, Peter Allen, our second son, was born at the Bethesda Naval Medical Center, Maryland at about 6:25 a.m. Peter was 8 lbs."

During this period, Jack spent many weeks at Norfolk Naval Base teaching intelligence, coming home to McLean on the weekends. Jack figured he was being groomed for his next big assignment. Being a navy weatherman was a great cover for any intelligence assignment!

Eventually, in August 1952, Jack became the Armed Forces Security Agency Unit Officer-in-Charge with forty-one personnel under his command. Jack's duties at the Armed Forces Security Agency mostly dealt with his team's electronic surveillance to capture and substantiate information, documentation and reporting of intelligence, and providing recommendations for counter-intelligence activities. Jack began to sense that an important new assignment was about to come.

Jack's twelfth great leadership character trait was *insight*!

Chapter Thirteen

No Such Agency

Jack's biggest assignment of all, based on global reach and international importance, came in the fall of 1952 when he was assigned Intelligence Officer-in-Charge of the National Security Agency Unit 2, located in Chicksands, Bedfordshire, England. The United States in 1950 had signed an agreement with England to set up a base called the 6940th Radio Squadron at Chicksands, which was responsible for continued communications and signal intelligence (SIGINT) operations while the U.S. Air Force and Navy SIGINT specialists were cracking Soviet codes.

Jack and his family deployed to the United Kingdom. This time Jack's adventures would include the whole family, and they were all eager. They arrived in Southampton on the SS *United States*, the fastest ocean liner of the day. The voyage alone was a grand adventure for the Ingram kids.

Upon arrival, it was not a coincidence that Jack's longtime navy friend, Charlie House, was at the dock to welcome them to England. Charlie was Jack's WWII aerologist hero friend who had been captured on Kiska Island after the Japanese invasion early in the war. Charlie had been a POW and, later, he was chosen by Navy Intelligence to spy on the Soviets with Jack.

1953 England photo ID (Karen, John, Doris, Bev & Pete)

Jack's orders coincided with President Truman signing a memorandum on October 24,

1952, that revised the National Security Council Intelligence Directive (NSCID) No. 9. Truman's memo was classified and the existence of the newly formed National Security Agency (NSA) was not known to the public at the time. Nor did Doris and the family know that Jack was attached to NSA or the significance of such duty. For months, NSA was referred to as "No Such Agency" by the U.S. intelligence community.

During this time in American history, everyone understood there was a state of Cold War existing between the United States and the Soviet Union and its satellite states, as well as with China and a few communist countries such as Cuba and Albania. Cold War meant no actual bloody warfare was going on because, in part, of the nuclear capabilities of the two "superpowers," the United States and the Soviet Union. The "balance of terror" concept guaranteed mutual annihilation if any country initiated a nuclear war.

There was little trust between the superpowers, and both used every means necessary to spy on the other. Jack's training and experience positioned him to be in the forefront and report back all these activities to Washington.

With a Top Secret/Crypto security clearance, Jack's communication and coordination included direct liaison responsibilities with the Joint Chiefs of Staff, Central Intelligence Agency, National Security Agency, USAF Security Service, and Army Security Service, since all Office of Naval Intelligence and other classified program problems, were, in effect, under his control at Chicksands. By 1956, he had fifty-one people reporting to him as the Officer-in Charge NSA Unit-2. Among other things, Jack's team's duties included monitoring and reporting on Soviet nuclear missile development activities.

During this time, the U.S. had few assets in the field. In the later days of Stalin's reign, the Iron Curtain had completely closed off the Soviet Union from CIA penetration—they had no agents of record in the U.S.S.R. Virtually the only asset available was SIGINT. Chicksands operated as a SIGINT collection site throughout WWII and long after the war, intercepting radio-transmitted traffic and passing the resulting

Family photo on the SS *United States* sailing to England

information along to help develop Cold War counterintelligence strategies and tactics. Hence, during this period, Jack Ingram became a Cold Warrior. Because of the high security of the assignment, Jack wrote virtually nothing in his journal about NSA Unit-2 and their activities. He was aware of the importance of his job as it related to national security.

One activity during this time was Project Genetrix, also known as WS-119L. Five hundred sixteen high-altitude "weather" balloons were launched from Norway, Scotland, Turkey, and Germany. These large, stratosphere-bound balloons were armed with heavy, classified state-of-the-art Polaroid cameras, designed to take photos from altitudes up to 100,000 feet. They were floated over the U.S.S.R. and Asia where forty-four were recovered and forty provided usable photographs. President Eisenhower was impressed that these huge balloons could effectively monitor such things as nuclear tests and return photography of more

Jack and Doris in England

than 1.1 million square miles of the Soviet bloc and China.

Aside from capturing important images of the U.S.S.R. for national security, Jack was able to capture and analyze vital meteorological data from these spy balloons, which became an invaluable source of operational information, and would later be used for safe and successful U2 plane reconnaissance spy missions.

The Ingram family settled into a nice way of life while in England. Their new home was at Coppice Mead Cottage on Brook Street, Stotfold, Bedfordshire, until July 1954. In 1955, they moved into a large estate home called Northfield House in the small village of Henlow, Bedfordshire. The children would have one year at an English public school, called a council school, in Henlow Village. Later, Karen and Bev were among the first students at Etonbury Academy, located on Stotfold Road, Arlesey, Bedfordshire.

The assignment in England was an excellent opportunity to expose the children to European travel so that they could see the places they had been reading about in their history books for years. It also afforded them the opportunity to visit their paternal ancestral homeland in Scotland.

During Easter of 1955, they made their first trip to Scotland, land of their forbears on the Ingram side, and enjoyed the trip very much. The weather was summer-like (in Scotland, it could have been quite cold and wet) and the scenery lovely.

Dad's Ingram side belonged to Clan Colquhoun, and he also had a bloodline of Dutch heritage (Jansen) on his maternal side. In the process of taking over 200 feet of film in color they found the name of Ingram or Clan Colquhoun at Loch Lomond. They also found Doris's heritage of the Burns family belonging to Clan Campbell. Jack and Doris learned about the battles between the Colquhoun and Campbell clans around Loch Lomond, which, for them, was very funny. The family spent a wonderful time at a local bed and breakfast and enjoyed swimming in the loch's cool waters.

Next, they visited Edinburgh, the capital, which was amazing with its vast King's Park and Arthur's Seat, Holyrood Palace, and the Royal Castle on the bluffs overlooking the city. The family did everything together and they had fun in the quaint places visited. They made use of Scottish bed-and-breakfast overnights. Moving very fast—Jack had limited time off—they covered all the main portions of Scotland in four days. The fresh mountain streams and falls, the mists and peace around the lochs, all combined to make a fabulous vacation.

In 1955, they traveled to Holland and Germany. Jack, Doris, Karen, Bev, John, and Pete left England on August 18. They crossed the English Channel to the Hook of Holland (Hoek van Holland) at night via ferry. It was a treat for the kids to sleep overnight on the ferry. The next morning, they boarded a train that carried them to Düsseldorf, where they transferred to another train that traveled along the Rhine River. Much time was spent staring out the windows of the train, catching glimpses of medieval castles sitting high above the river.

One of the cities they saw was Cologne. It was a horrible sight because it had not been rebuilt since WWII. Bonn and Koblenz were the same. For the Ingram family, these sights were a shock. They had been mostly insulated from the ravages of the war. Even for Jack, who had been instrumental in the efforts of the Pacific theater of WWII, the bombed-out buildings were a terrible sight. Jack patiently answered his children's questions about what had occurred there not so long before.

One of the highlights of the trip for the children was eating in the diner car with the whole family. They were waited on royally and served a delicious meal. For Jack and Doris, it was an opportunity to reinforce in their children the importance of good manners. "Sit up straight, John," Jack scolded, as Doris instructed Karen and Beverly how to place their napkins on their laps and hold their knives and forks properly.

They slept on the train that night before arriving in Garmisch-Partenkirchen in Bavaria, south of Munich. They had traveled through Stuttgart before arriving and were very conscious of the change of scenery. Many of the buildings looked like chalets, and some of the people were clothed in traditional Bavarian garb.

The family visited landmarks and took bus tours to explore the area. One of the trips was to the stately Linderhof Palace, with its enormous gardens and walkways. It was the home of King Ludwig II. The front of the estate had a large, incredible fountain. Jack was so impressed with it, he used up much of his film on his movie camera. Another excursion was to the Neuschwanstein Castle, also built for King Ludwig II, above the village of Hohenschwangau. The king died in 1886, and the castle was opened to the public.

The next day Jack planned an excursion to the top of the Zugspitze, in the Alps, which required taking a cog train. The cog train rode on a track but was also equipped with a gear under the train that connected to a corresponding tooth-cut rod in the middle of the tracks. This allowed the train the reinforcement necessary to "climb" the mountain. Needless to say, it was a slow trip!

Upon boarding the train there were not enough available seats together to accommodate the whole Ingram family, so Karen, the oldest, at not-quite thirteen, was placed next to a stranger, a very nice lady. Being a bit shy and not speaking German, Karen was nervous sitting down. But the nice lady right away started asking all kinds of questions in English: Where do you live? Where in the states? Where in England? How many in the family? Where do you go to school? What does your father do? Karen happily answered the woman's many questions, not realizing that her father was watching and listening carefully to every word.

Ingram family at Northfield House home in Bedfordshire

When the train arrived at a midway station as a rest stop, Jack pulled his daughter aside. Bending down low to her face, and in a very strong, low, hard whisper he said, "What is the matter with you? You cannot be telling people our business! You have no idea who that person is, and you never know what that could mean for your family. Your whole family!"

Karen had never seen her father so angry, and she began to cry. Trying only to be polite, she couldn't quite understand that she had done something so wrong.

Jack comforted his daughter and explained that the work he did was for the good and safety of the United States and England. He made it clear that it was secret work and he was not even able to tell his family about it. He explained that many other people were spies and you could never tell who the spies were. In a much milder tone, he asked Karen, "You want to be free, right? You want your family to be free and to be able to return to McLean, right?" Karen, of course, violently nodded her head in the affirmative!

For Karen, it was a memorable lesson. She realized that Dad didn't just go to work, he worked so others could be free to work.

The Ingram family spent a most enjoyable week visiting castles, lakes, shops, and churches with an exhilarating ride to the top of the Zugspitze, at over 10,000 feet, the highest of the Alps in Germany. With the kids watching and Jack shooting film, Doris actually climbed to the Zugspitze summit with a climbing line hitched around her waist.

Jack took 600 feet of color 8-millimeter film on that trip. What his family did not know was that, before the trip, he had the Model 605TA Viceroy movie camera fitted with a special state-of-the-art "critical focuser" lens on April 4 in preparation for the trip. Was he taking film footage of the Alps' geography that high-altitude spy balloons would have to clear later in the year? And, coincidentally, one of the U.S. Air Force Secret Service listening posts sending intelligence to Chicksands was located in Landsberg am Lech, Germany, near where the family vacationed.

In late September 1956, the family sailed for New York from Southampton, and then they traveled on to McLean, Virginia. Soon after arriving back in the United States, Jack bought a two-toned blue Chevrolet that he nicknamed the "Bonnie Blue Bell."

In October of that year, Jack received orders to run the FLEET WEATHER CENTRAL in Norfolk, Virginia. He had been selected as a navy lieutenant commander and in his journal he proclaimed, "Thanks to God!" He had twenty-eight people under his command where he, once again, had been given split responsibilities for Atlantic fleet weather forecasting and navy intelligence collection, interpretation, and dissemination.

While in Norfolk, Jack wrote a scientific Top Secret classified paper called, "Transosonde" for the military. It was a thorough description of the navy research lab's latest high-altitude stratosphere weather and intelligence balloons that carried aloft weather instruments and spy camera payloads to record valuable data on immediate conditions of atmospheric pressure, temperature, humidity, and wind speed. It utilized radiosonde instrument technology tracked by radar and other radio direction-finding devices. Jack was responsible for seeing that most of these "weather" balloons carried spy cameras for capturing images of the U.S.S.R. Of course, like his time in England, he used these balloons for collecting high-altitude photographic reconnaissance images.

After participating in the U.S. Navy Review in Norfolk—the 350th anniversary of the U.S. Navy, Jack took his family on several trips to key historic sites in the United States. In the fall of 1957, the family visited historic Jamestown, near Williamsburg, Virginia. Coming from the West Coast these East Coast historical sites were new and fascinating to them.

They also toured the Blue Ridge Mountains and Skyline Drive, and in November they took a trip to Kitty Hawk, North Carolina. There they visited the site of Orville and Wilbur Wrights' monumental accomplishment, the first manned, heavier-than-air flight and proof that man could fly with the help of a machine. Next, they ventured down the road to Roanoke Colony, also known as the Lost Colony, on Roanoke Island, and then continued down to the sand spits of Cape Hatteras and the little town named Hatteras.

The Ingram family traveled quite a bit during this period, and the older children were at an age when they could remember and appreciate the travel. Each place they visited, Jack enjoyed teaching his kids the historical significance of the sites. The children learned a great deal about the history and the culture of different places. But for Karen, the most important lesson was the one she had learned in Germany.

Jack's thirteenth great leadership character trait was *confidentiality*!

Chapter Fourteen

Seasoned Sailor

On August 10, 1957, Jack was present for the commissioning of the new Forrestal-Class supercarrier USS *Ranger* CVA-61 at Newport News, Virginia. The USS *Ranger* was the first carrier planned and engineered to be built with an angled deck. Three other carriers in the fleet had angled decks, but they were design changes after construction commenced. Jack admired the size and beauty of the ship, a virtual floating city.

In late December of that year, Jack was selected to report for duty on USS *Ranger* as its first aerology officer and intelligence officer. His unit consisted of eighteen personnel and many navy ROTC staff. He reported to USS *Ranger* under the command of Captain Charles T. Booth. On January 16, they sailed for Guantánamo Bay, Cuba. New jets flew off the deck for the *Ranger*'s first high-speed tests and gun practice. The *Ranger* was the most sophisticated vessel in the U.S. Navy!

Beyond overseeing his team of aerologists to produce accurate forecasts for operations at sea, Jack also served as intelligence officer, legal officer, and public relations liaison for Captain Booth. Often he would be flown to shore with a reconnaissance landing party of officers and marines to set up a schedule for Captain Booth's visits with dignitaries. In his spare time, he helped as a boxing coach for young sailors aboard ship.

In March 1958, USS *Ranger* had a new captain assigned to her. Captain Paul Buie took command, and, in July, the *Ranger* sailed on a two-month goodwill cruise from Norfolk, Virginia, to Alameda, California, around Cape Horn at the southernmost tip of South America. Jack had several navy ROTC men under his command that had never been on board a ship. He was a good mentor and taught them a great deal about being a sailor beyond what any school could offer. Stops to meet with dignitaries were made at Rio de Janeiro, Brazil; Valparaíso, Chile; Callao, Peru; and Acapulco, Mexico. While in port, Jack's boxing team would take on the local boxers. The *Ranger*'s boxing team was young and inex-

USS Ranger at sea - 1958

perienced, and they would often get "whipped." Jack told them the South American boxers were professional boxers and were very good!

The seas and weather sailing around "the Horn" were known to be among the roughest in the world. Fortunately, storms anticipated were never encountered, although Jack documented, "A blow while at anchor off Valparaíso, Chile, was considerable." Otherwise the weather on the trip was uneventful. On the cruise Jack wrote a paper titled, "Sixty Days of Weather Round the Horn." It was well received by Captain Buie and Jack's weather colleagues throughout the fleet.

On the 20th of August 1958, the *Ranger* arrived at Alameda, California, and Jack was reunited, in his words, "with my wonderful family."

Doris, Beverly, Karen, Johnny, and Peter, as well as Jack's older sister Mary, were all waiting for him at the dock. While Jack was at sea, Doris and the family traveled across the country to join Jack.

The USS *Ranger* was now in its new home port of Naval Air Station Alameda, where the Ingram family would live for the time being. August and September were a hectic training period for Jack. Aboard the *Ranger*, the flight crew trained by flying hundreds of sorties, staying in a state of readiness that Jack had experienced many years ago. The difference was that the planes were new jets compared to the biplanes of the late 1930s that he had flown on and off "Lady Lex," the old *Lexington* CV-2.

Jack was once again able to be close to his family for a few months, although the training aboard the *Ranger* kept him busy and away from home a lot. He soon received notification that the *Ranger* would be heading out after the first of the year, but at least he would be able to spend the holidays with his family.

Following intensive training for all aboard the *Ranger*, she set sail again for the western Pacific. Once again, Jack was leaving his family. He was supposed to return by July 22 after training, exercises, and goodwill visits in Japan. Pearl Harbor was the first stop on January 9. In 1959, the *Ranger* was now operating in the Hawaiian Islands. Jack missed his family more than ever. With four children growing like weeds he was aware of how much of their lives he was missing.

Jack attended a briefing by Admiral Fells, Commander in Chief, Pacific Fleet (CINCPAC), and about the importance of the western Pacific (WESTPAC) cruise. The briefing reminded Jack of his days on board the *Catoctin* after WWII when he learned how to collect intelligence and write briefs for Washington. Now Jack was teaching others how to collect, interpret, and disseminate intelligence. He thought to himself, "as much as things change, they are always the same."

On the 14th of February, Valentine's Day, the *Ranger* departed Pearl Harbor for Yokosuka, Japan. Jack could not help but think of Doris; she had sent word that she was, once again, going to have another baby. If estimations were correct, he should be home just in time for the birth. As

PR officer, Jack kept himself busy, setting up important meetings with Japanese dignitaries including dinner meetings for the captain and his staff, Jack included, with ex-Japanese military officers and the Japanese royal family. No love was lost between Jack and the Japanese delegation, but he made the best out of his responsibility to represent the best of the navy and his country.

On February 23, USS *Ranger* arrived off Tokyo Bay. Jack said in his journal, "Doris wrote and told me of almost losing the baby. She is ok now. Please God keep them safe. Thy Love!"

On March 10, they arrived at Hong Kong, British Crown Colony, and the sampan boats were everywhere! In late March, USS *Ranger* had another change of command at sea with Noel Gayler becoming the *Ranger*'s third captain in two years. Jack's duties did not change, and he knew Gayler from his time working at the Pentagon in navy intelligence and also years earlier when Gayler was an aviator on USS *Lexington*. Gayler was the first navy pilot in history to be awarded the Navy Cross three times. Jack had great respect for him. As Captain of the *Ranger*, Gayler was given the challenge to work on developing an aircraft carrier strike force that would be prepared for operations in a potential nuclear theater of war.

Gayler was more demonstrative than the *Ranger*'s previous captains, and he acted on Jack's forecasts for air strike operations. Gayler liked to be informed and he always took decisive action! In an unclassified document to Gayler, Jack wrote the following "situation" memorandum:

"Situation

"The attack aircraft carrier is at sea and a nuclear weapons strike is to be conducted against a specific target in enemy territory. As determined by the officer in command, two alternative targets are required and the following must be considered:

"(a) Enemy redeploys and evacuates in specific target area, or;

"(b) Severe weather conditions exist over specific target and no foreseeable changes are forecast, or;

"(c) Superior enemy forces have strengthened specific target.

Jack with his USS *Ranger* unit on board ship

"The Meteorological Officer must prepare and present adequate meteorological data to support the foregoing strike covering flights projecting 700 miles on the outbound leg to the North, West, and South.

"The reconnaissance flights preceding the strike will cover approximately 2,500 miles (round robins).

"The Meteorological Officer must recommend launch areas within strike range of all three targets that will provide suitable weather conditions for launch, concealment if possible, and reliable aircraft recovery areas—all free of nuclear fallout contamination.

"In all, forecasters must evaluate incoming weather information covering over a million square miles. The evaluation must enable the meteorological officer to present:

Jack exhibiting "good will" in the state room with Japanese officers from WWII

WARDROOM
SERVICE CAPTAIN
BARBER T SD1

"(a) Pre-strike,

"(b) Strike,

"(c) Post-strike,

"(d) and, Reconnaissance weather information

"Quick reaction capability of a strike commander requires launch of all 'up' mission aircraft immediately. In the tactical situation then, mission pilots stand by in the ready rooms (at least 6 including intelligence) and must be launched in pre-loaded aircraft in 4 minutes or less. Obviously, there is no time for any last minute briefing. The only alternative, under the present briefing setup, is to continually update weather and intelligence data pertaining to the strike as it becomes available.

"The present system of 'updating' weather information is a distortion of the facts. Surface Synoptic weather information is generated at six hour intervals only. Upper air information (vital to jet speeds, altitudes, performance) is only available every twelve hours.

"Airways sequences are the most frequent broadcast measurements of weather as they are made hourly. The sequences are used, when reception permits, to update weather information briefings in the ready rooms.

"All of the foregoing (surface synoptic, upper air and hourly) weather information is processed by hand plotters, hand analyzers, and a hand writing forecaster. The process takes one and one-half hours after observation time. The plotter takes another hour and the analyst at least three fourths of an hour. An experienced forecaster will require another half hour to write the forecast for ONE STRIKE—THE FORECASTERS MAY HAVE SIX!

"This detailed processing by hand can thus vary from 3.75 hours up to 6.75 hours (after observation) depending on the magnitude of the mission.

"It ties up the most experienced meteorologist who should be personally briefing the strike commander and pilots for the mission.

"It is firmly established that the commander of an impending strike force operation must be ready to accept an equivocal weather prediction from his meteorologist, for weather forecasts that are correct 100% of the time are not possible, nor are they likely to be in the foreseeable future.

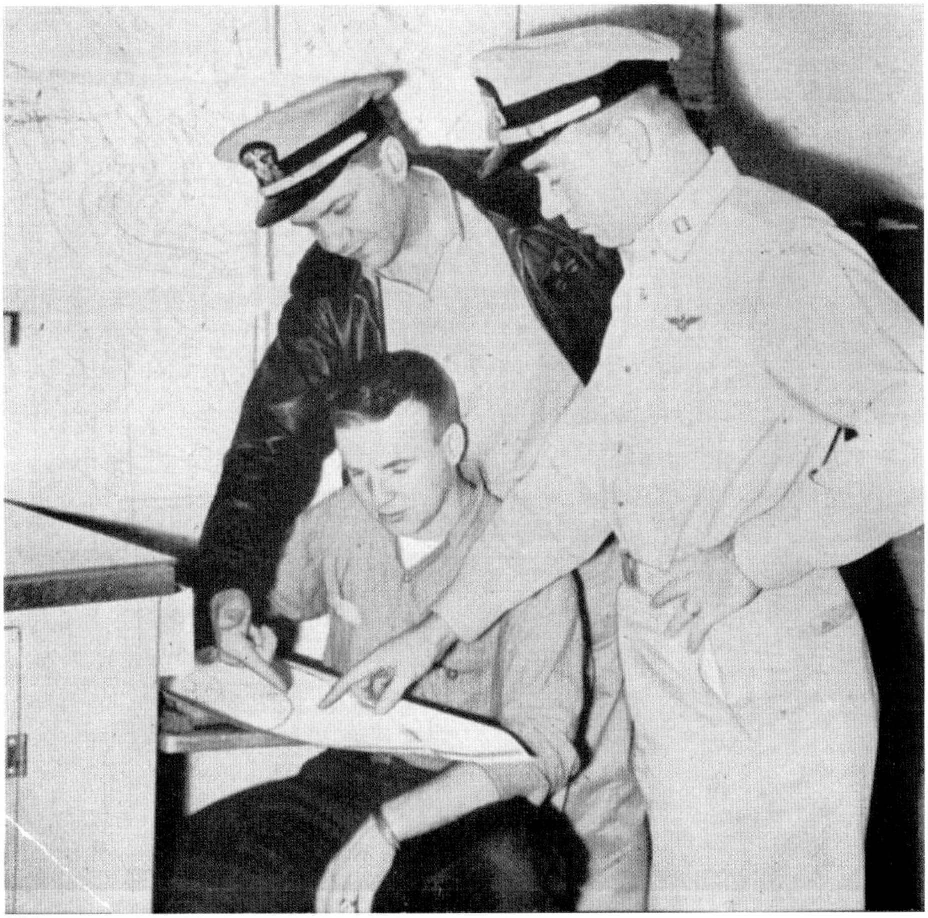

Jack's aerologists preparing forecast for USS Ranger operations

"Having struggled through the foregoing, while conducting briefings, prior to completion of a proper analysis and/or forecast (which is tenuous at best), the command decision is made; hopefully with God's aid on the one hand, or a rabbit's foot in the pocket, or a sense of buoyancy from having won last night's poker game.

"The strike is launched! The roar of jet vibrations and spirits run high—then silence. The die is cast.

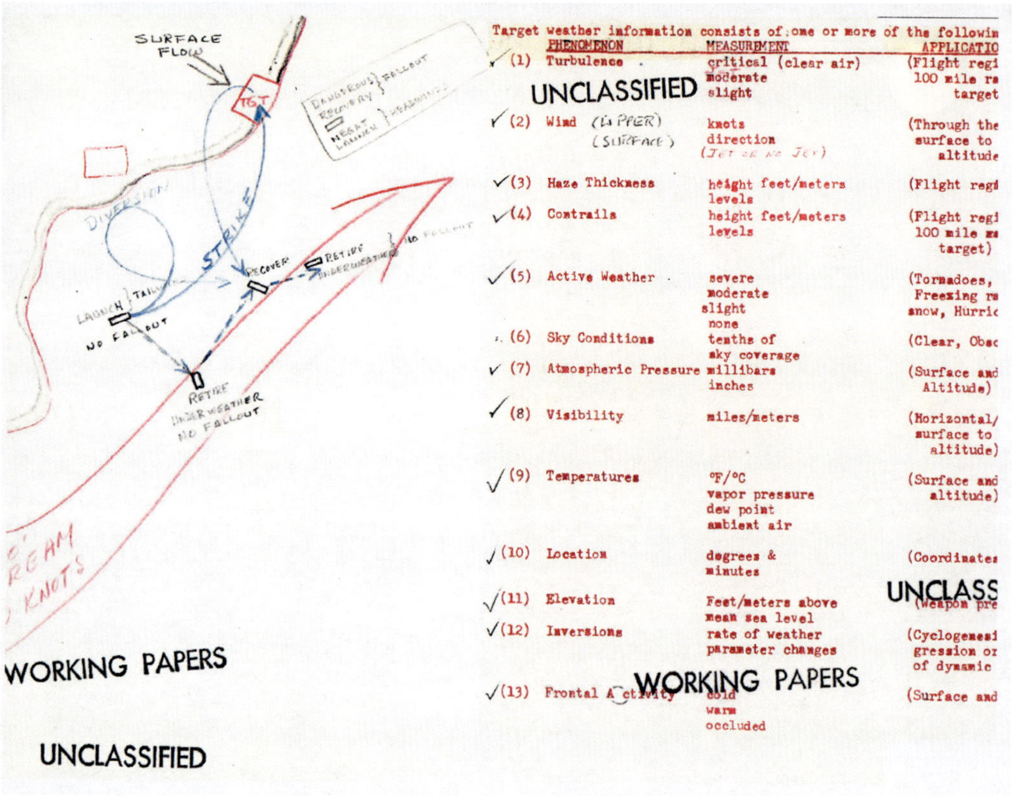

Jack's drawing of a carrier nuclear strike mission

"Just before the strike returns (if they return) the master central of all knowledge comes through with facsimile photos of the entire Pacific, or Atlantic Oceans giving static weather picture analysis, prognoses, etc., usually unreliable, garbled and TOO LATE!

"By this time, often as much a 7 to 8 hours after observation, the facsimile pictures relate only history!!

"The best weather information at this point is obtained by debriefing the returning pilots who were there just 20 minutes ago. Pilots are excellent at affirming good or bad weather data, and they often have a tendency to blame poor navigation on bad wind data. So, clear and honest communication is extremely important amongst the pilots and meteorologist. Trust is the key!

"If the forecast is wrong the loss of pilot confidence can be disastrous—not just for the meteorologist—the whole air group will suddenly develop mechanical, radio, or electronic problems downing one third of the aircraft.

"If the forecast is correct the forecaster rides a short-lived popularity, as the meteorological officer's team can't maintain that batting average.

"The tempo of such operations, seriously, are demanding in the extreme. The psychological factors involved, alone, in some cases overwhelm pilots. Pilots grounded during uncertain weather conditions, poor weather communication support, or when scheduled for a touchy strike situation would warrant a study in itself. Pilots that try to use weather information spend a great deal of their time with the meteorological officer and they know when the forecast is fact, 'a guess', or 'hope.'

"Oh yes. Then there's the wise guy. An otherwise excellent strike condition can be clobbered by an Air Group Commander (believe it or not).

"For example:

"Your reconnaissance (RECCO) which the commander of Carrier X ordered, allows you to lock on a firm 48 hour confirmation of satisfactory weather for all strike areas. The air group commander orders a combat air patrol (CAP) to fly his own RECCO, and reports on return weather conditions being unsatisfactory. The whole operation is stagnated, pilots abort, and you wonder what the hell the war is all about. Who's fighting who? Air group commanders that don't value the opinion of the meteorological officer sends the air group into a state of flux."

From the memo, Jack certainly had open dialogue with Gayler about new aircraft carrier strategy and tactics to forecast missions during possible nuclear warfare. Gayler appreciated candor and incorporated many of Jack's meteorological and operational recommendations into air operations.

Ranger pilots and Fleet air group commanders, working with Jack and his aerographers, codified the rules of aircraft carrier strike force

Jack coaching Ranger boxers (right side of ring)

weather protocol in the early 1960s. They were now not only forecasting for strike force bombing missions, but they had to also forecast for protecting the ship, aircraft, and pilots from nuclear blasts and associated radioactive fallout.

Gayler allowed Jack to work closely with air group commanders by collaborating on ways to parse the elements of weather to ensure successful missions. Jack's experience with pilots and weather from flying cold WWII Aleutian bombing missions to hazardous hurricane-hunting duty in the Atlantic gave new jet pilots the confidence they needed for the day.

During this time, Jack would establish a new direction for instant forecasting on the *Ranger* by broadcasting the first televised forecast on board a navy ship for pilots in the ready room.

After Jack and Gayler created a better plan for flight weather certainty, *Ranger* then left Hong Kong for Okinawa and on to Ryukyu Island for more flight operations. Sadly, though, they lost two A3D officers and one FHD pilot during flight operations. The catapult on the *Ranger* was something that some pilots could not master. Sometimes pilots would panic and not trust the massive catapult thrust and push for more power off the deck only to fly straight into the ocean—never to return.

Jack received a communication from navy command indicating that his next tour of duty would be in Washington D.C. Jack hoped that he would have some stable time back in McLean with his family. Gayler was instrumental in getting Jack his orders to return back home and to the Pentagon for other missions brewing in navy intelligence.

Jack awarding a first place trophy to a fellow boxing coach

In mid-April, on his arrival at Sasebo, Japan, Jack visited Nagasaki on tour, the site of the second atomic bombing of Japan during WWII. Although rebuilding was extensive, the gravity of visiting the site was not lost on Jack. Some of the men under his command had been small boys during WWII, and Jack had to fill them in on what the war was like for navy men.

By the 22nd of April, the ship stopped at Okinawa again. "Fly, fly, fly," Jack wrote in his journal, "One special test after another." They departed the same day for the waters off Taiwan.

The *Ranger* continued its fast-paced island hopping. It was a nostalgic day for Jack when he recorded in his journal, "28 April. Arrived Manila Bay again after 18 years. Hot, sticky, and stinking—no change. President of the Philippines host F8 saved pilot - Just Ok - 29 April." In early May, USS *Ranger* arrived and departed Subic Bay, which was a big, super-jet base.

Jack giving Captain Lockhart's grandson, Geoffrey, a tour of the Ranger

Jack's USS Ranger yearbook photo

By the 5th of June, they were sailing back to Yokosuka, Japan. On his free time, Jack wrote, "I took the Imperial family on board ship in terrible weather, but all turned out ok. Bad conditions prevailed but show must go on!" Then he wrote, "Taking tour to Tokyo tomorrow for pictures. Rain is expected, but tour includes a chorus show, which I'm going to try to get on film. We sail for home next month. If I can only get back before the newcomer is born." Doris was expecting their fifth baby in August, and Jack wanted more than anything to be there.

On the fourth of July, Independence Day, the crew had a memorial service for the men of another A3D twin-jet bomber that crashed at sea. Jack wrote, "One of the officers was married with three children, and a chief, also with three kids, survived. One bachelor. These recent losses bring to mind how dangerous service still is, even in the peacetime navy. Death out here is a guard of free people." Then, quoting from Thomas Campbell's poem "Hallowed Ground," "To live in hearts we leave behind / Is not to die."

Jack's wings and medal ribbons

The memorial service only increased the ache in Jack's heart. He wrote, "Just nine days before we set sail for home. Supposed to arrive San Francisco on 28 July. Now heading to Okinawa to drop off staff to the carrier *Shangri La*. Sure hope to get back before Doris has the baby."

As the days and miles passed, Jack became ever more anxious to see his family, "On the 15th of July, we passed chop from 7th fleet. Hooray! July 17th – Passed 180th Meridian. Hooray! Normal exercises at Pearl and home by 27th or 28th – Oh, how time can carry on and on when away from loved ones!"

"Great day! Great Joy! It's July 27th and a happy day!" The *Ranger* had finally arrived home at Alameda! Doris, Karen, Beverly, John, and little Peter were there to greet him, and all were fine!

Jack did indeed make it home in time. On the 18th of August 1959, James Burns Ingram was born in fine shape at Oak Knoll Naval Hospital in Oakland, California. James was baptized on October 24 at St. Barnabas Church, Alameda, California.

The *Ranger* stayed close to San Francisco Bay for a while, operating up and down the Pacific coast. Jack invited Captain Lockhart (USN Retired) and his grandson, Geoffrey, on board for luncheon and tour of the ship. Captain Lockhart was an early commander and was influential in Jack's career before, during, and after WWII. Jack wrote in his journal, "Captain Lockhart gave me a start in the U.S. Navy over 24 years ago." Jack often invited Doris and the kids aboard the *Ranger* for Sunday brunches in Alameda. They all quickly became friends with Admiral Gayler. Noel Gayler was about the same age as Jack, and they shared family values.

Gayler admired Jack for his rise through the ranks as a "maverick" and Jack respected Gayler for his ability to allow his officers to run the ship.

Later that year, however, tragedy struck again. Jack wrote, "The *Ranger* lost an A4D plane off a deck cat shot. Another pilot has been killed, and he was the 8th death in flight operations over 2 years and 4 months." He went on to say, "May God have mercy on their souls—bobbing on floating wing tank for a tombstone!"

On the 29th of November, Lieutenant Cliff Samples reported aboard the *Ranger* as Jack's aerology relief officer. Two other officers were needed to replace him in the realms of intelligence and legal duties.

Captain Gayler gave Jack a commendation for WESTPAC performance of duty, for which Jack was very proud.

Moreover, Gayler was compelled to write the following recommendation for Jack's selection for commander:

"LCDR Ingram, in over a quarter century of constant superior naval service, is recognized as a most outstanding, aggressive and versatile officer in all phases of Naval Meteorology, Special Naval Intelligence and Aviation Operations.

"He has repeatedly demonstrated outstanding ability, with tact and a "can-do" attitude as a U.S. Navy Field Operational Intelligence Officer in coordinating and effecting fulfillment of Navy operational intelligence and numerous other classified projects and missions.

"In most cases, LCDR Ingram's coordination included serving as a liaison with the Joint Chiefs of Staff, Central Intelligence Agency,

National Security Agency, USAF Security Service, and Army Security Service. Ingram's ingenuity in his present assignment reflects his valued professional and varied military experience in most Naval areas on a worldwide basis.

"As a result of LCDR Ingram's superior planning briefs, recommendations and methods of implementation, the Naval Operating Forces today possess a more realistic and flexible fleet readiness posture than ever before in Naval history. His briefings rank as the best I have observed, particularly in content, organization and quality. His accomplishment has gained him recognition, by his commanding officers, and he has been nominated for the Outstanding Contribution Award of the Naval Weather Service.

"To summarize, LCDR Ingram is a leader of proven ability, initiative, competence, loyalty, willingness and know-how whose performance of all duty has been accomplished in an outstanding manner. Such attributes characterize his high caliber and fitness for greater responsibility in the Naval Service.

"Therefore, in view of his vast and unique Naval experience, proven outstanding leadership in operational assignments afloat and ashore and his previously described areas of importance to the readiness posture of the operational forces, U.S. Fleet, I believe that LCDR Ingram compares most favorably with commanders of the line and is without reservation strongly recommended for promotion to Commander."

Jack had orders to return east again to Washington D.C. In October, Jack purchased a Volkswagen camper that the family named the "JB" in honor of young James Burns, and just after the holidays they set out across the country once again.

Jack was ordered to the Navy Field Operational Intelligence Office, Fort George G. Meade, Maryland—NSA. He was the chief weather officer, but he also had secret duties that he could not discuss.

In March of that year, Doris and Jack were given a surprise birthday party by their friends in McLean. Jack's and Doris's birthdays were one day apart, on the 15th and 16th of March. Jack was 46 and Doris

Jack and Doris at retirement ceremony presentation with Rear Admiral Samual B. Frankel, Chief of Staff, Defense Intelligence Agency

40! Unfortunately, there had been many years when they were unable to celebrate their birthdays together.

Karen graduated from high school in June and worked for the telephone company as an operator as she worked her way through Marymount University pursuing a degree in education. Bev worked at the telephone company as well while she attended Bishop Denis J. O'Connell High School. John and Pete went to St. John's Elementary School. The children were growing up so fast!

By September 1961, Jack was beginning to feel some frustrations on the job. He wrote, "Job with ONI is a real challenge." He now had to deal with Cold War politics. Vital navy intelligence and operational advice would be considered, but security agency intelligence recommendations were not always followed. More and more, the Kennedy administration made its own decisions based on politics and not recommendations from the CIA, NSA, and Office of Naval Intelligence (ONI). Before 1960, he really liked working for President Eisenhower because Ike was an intelligence visionary. Jack said, "Ike would look at the analysis, consider all the facts, and always follow the recommendations from the intelligence information gathered by our team."

A clear example of Kennedy's different approach surfaced during the failed Bay of Pigs invasion of Cuba. In March 1960, Eisenhower authorized the CIA to organize an invasion to oust the communist Cuban government of Fidel Castro, which had close ties with the Soviet Union. The CIA had prepared by setting up camps in Guatemala to train Cuban exiles for an invasion to retake their homeland. By November's presidential election, the CIA operation had trained a small army for an assault landing and guerilla warfare.

After his inauguration in January, Kennedy agreed to the final invasion plan, but he decided to provide only half the forces our U.S. intelligence agencies suggested were necessary to be successful. Eisenhower's original invasion plan included both air and naval support that had been recommended by the intelligence agencies. The only air support came on April 15 when eight CIA-sponsored, obsolete WWII B-26 bombers, that were painted to resemble Cuban air force planes, left Nicaragua to bomb Cuban airfields and other army installations, but they were ordered by Kennedy to come back to the United States never to return for subsequent missions.

On April 16 Kennedy pulled all air cover for the land invasion and the CIA-trained Cuban counter-revolutionary forces surrendered on April 20. The failed invasion only strengthened the relationship between Castro and the U.S.S.R., eventually leading to the Cuban Missile Crisis of 1962.

During this time, Jack did not always agree with Kennedy and his administration. He was frustrated by the administration being "smarter"

Ingram Family - 1963 (John, Bev, Karen, & Pete standing; Jack, Jim, Doris & Mary Etta sitting)

than his hardworking intelligence staff. Nevertheless, Jack worked diligently and received two commendations from Captain Tatom for his intelligence work during and after the failed Bay of Pigs invasion.

On July 1, 1963, in an unassuming way, Jack wrote, "Completed 28 years 2 months of naval service and retired from U.S. Navy as lieutenant commander." Typical of Jack, this was not a lot of acknowledgement for a long and dedicated career in the navy. He had traveled and served his county across the globe, in horrific weather conditions in the Aleutians, through WWII, flying into hurricanes, and used his practical experience in weather and intelligence to help develop the next generation of our country's defenders. Jack demonstrated many times over his dedication to the navy, his country, and, most of all, to his family.

Over his many years of service, Jack was designated a naval aviator observer, given his wings, and he earned the following awards and decorations exemplifying fidelity and obedience to the navy:

- Air Medal
- Good Conduct Medal with 3 gold stars
- China Service Medal
- American Defense Medal (Fleet)
- American Campaign Medal
- Asiatic Pacific Campaign Medal
- World War II Victory Medal
- Navy Occupation Medal
- National Defense Service Medal

Jack's fourteenth great leadership character trait was *dedication*!

Chapter Fifteen

Tireless Patriot

On the July 8, 1963, Dad started employment with HRB-Singer, Inc., State College, Pennsylvania. HRB was an engineering firm working on government contracts for the navy, NSA, and other government agencies. Jack's high-security clearance and his contacts with ONI, the navy, the air force, the Pentagon, CIA, and NSA were attractive for HRB to hire him as a proposal writer and liaison.

Jack and Doris bought a house in State College, within walking distance of the State College Area High School and The Pennsylvania State University. Jack recalled how much he had liked the landscape of Pennsylvania on his train trip across the country so many decades before.

The home was fantastically located for a young family to further their education. The three boys ran track and played football, baseball, and basketball. They were also very active in the community, serving as altar boys at Our Lady of Victory Church and joining the Boy Scouts in Boalsburg, Pennsylvania.

Jack, President of HRB Singer's Employee Benefit Organization donating funds to the hospital

Doris was by now expecting their sixth child and, on the 21st of October, Mary Etta was born at Bethesda Naval Hospital, by emergency Caesarian section. In his journal, Jack wrote, "Doris and Mary Etta did okay!" Mary Etta was a fortunate little girl because she, in essence, had three mothers with both Karen and Bev eager to help Mom with motherly duties when they were not working or going to school. Karen also worked for HRB and Bev had enrolled at Penn State. Later, Bev took time off from her college classes to work full time at HRB like her sister. John and Pete worked at Weis Markets part time while in high school, and after turning eight years of age, young Jim worked cutting grass around the neighborhood. Jack and Doris had two major rules for their children: 1) they had to pay for their own car insurance; 2) they had to pay for their own college education.

Jack and Jim - 1965

During the 1960s, Jack wrote many government proposals and delivered them to government agencies in Washington, securing large contracts for HRB. He frequently traveled to Washington for meetings but once again, could not talk about his work privately. He also made several trips to Texas in the fall of 1963. Records indicate that they were mostly intelligence advisory roles for the USAF Secret Service (USAFSS) in El Paso.

In addition to his work at HRB, Jack was, at times, called up by the government for occasional intelligence duty, even though he was retired. Doris and the children thought the secret life of a naval intelligence officer was over. Jack thought that he would have unlimited time to travel, renew old acquaintances, and spend time with the family. But his life continued to be consumed with secret work with private government contractors working on the Vietnam War effort and other never-discussed missions.

In November of 1966, Jack and Doris bought Bonnie Glen, which Jack described as "80 acres of God's country," near Woodward, Pennsylvania. They found the property after looking many years for a place to enjoy out in the country. While the entire family was still together, they would travel the countryside around State College looking at properties on Sunday drives. Bonnie Glen met all of Jack and Doris's requirements:

1) It had to have its own spring-fed water source;

2) It had to have an abundance of wildlife;

3) It had to have its own mineral rights;

4) It had to be at least 50 acres of combination mountain forest and field meadow land; and

5) It had to be close to State College.

Bonnie Glen was situated at the foot of Woodward Mountain in a pretty (bonnie) little valley (glen), within Penns Valley between the villages of Coburn and Woodward. For the children growing up, it was the best of a lot of worlds! Seven springs flowed from the mountain, feeding a beautiful stream and the meadows. Deer, bear, turkey, grouse, rabbit, and squirrel from the land, and trout from the stream, were plentiful. The children could ride a pony, hunt, fish, and run all over the mountains that surrounded the property. The Ingram family began raising beagles and chickens.

In October of 1971, with much nostalgia, Jack and Doris sold their first home, the beautiful little rambler in McLean, Virginia. They had rented out the property for eight years and wanted to move on from the burdens of maintaining the house.

Jack's reputation for securing war-related government contracts and non-war-related engineering contracts became well known in the early 1970s around Penn State and the State College community. He also worked for a new company named C-COR Electronics, a pioneer in amplifiers for cable TV transmission and other cutting-edge engineering endeavors. Jack helped Jim Palmer, C-COR's owner and president, secure many contracts.

Woodbadge leadership - Jack is on the left with standard

He became C-COR's public relations officer in charge of marketing as well.

One time, Jack hired Jesse Owens, the track star and 1936 Olympic gold medalist, to help advertise C-COR's products at conventions around the country. Jesse was just a few years older than Jack and they got along famously because they were both of the same depression-era generation and self-made men.

There was one spring day when Jack brought Jesse out to one of young Jim's track meets at the Westerly Parkway Junior High track in State College. Jim was on the junior high team—sprinting, hurdling, and long jumping that day.

Jim was lining up at the starting line to sprint when Jack and Jesse walked up behind the crowd of boys on the infield of the track. The starter pistol fired and off they went! "Go, Ingy! Go!" the boys shouted as Jim sprinted down the track. Jack couldn't help but feel a special kind of pride because "Ingy" was what his buddies aboard the *Pennsylvania* had called him so many years ago.

The boys and coaches couldn't believe that Jesse Owens would take the time to visit with them! He watched them compete and gave great pointers about good running and long-jumping technique. He signed autographs and gave some of the best advice about both track and life that a professional track athlete could convey. Jack was certainly a hero to his son and the other boys that day!

In October of 1972, Jack was working for Locus, Inc., another engineering firm in Boalsburg near State College. He had maintained his professional contacts and created numerous new relationships with engineering firms around State College. Locus was one of his favorite companies because its leadership allowed Jack the latitude he needed to help the company build their brand.

Jack respected Bob Riddle, cofounder of Locus. Bob and Jack had known each other since 1963, from working together at HRB-Singer. Bob had directed the activities of the electromagnetic systems division in the design and development of airborne, spaceborne, and ground-based electronic SIGINT systems. Bob was a genius who coauthored a book about transistor physics and circuits and was granted a patent on a proportional gate circuit in 1958. Bob simulated the radiation environment of space in the research reactor at Penn State and studied the effects of nuclear radiation on transistors and other components. He supervised the design and construction of automatic electric intercept systems. Bob was a WWII and Korea air force secret service veteran and he admired Jack for his navy, ONI, NSA, and USAFSS intelligence background, working with SIGINT systems before, during, and after WWII. Jack wrote many technical publications for Bob, which explained breakthroughs and advancements in technology and new secret electronics systems. They were good friends who shared a common classified language of spying and national security!

With his boys at an impressionable age in the years between 1963 and 1973, Jack became highly involved with Scouting. He was well known for his willingness to help young men in the Boy Scouts, serving as an assistant Scout master in Boalsburg and then as Scout master at Our Lady of Victory Church in State College.

Jack took everything he did seriously. Before becoming a Scout master, he took a weeklong course for Scouting leaders called Wood Badge.

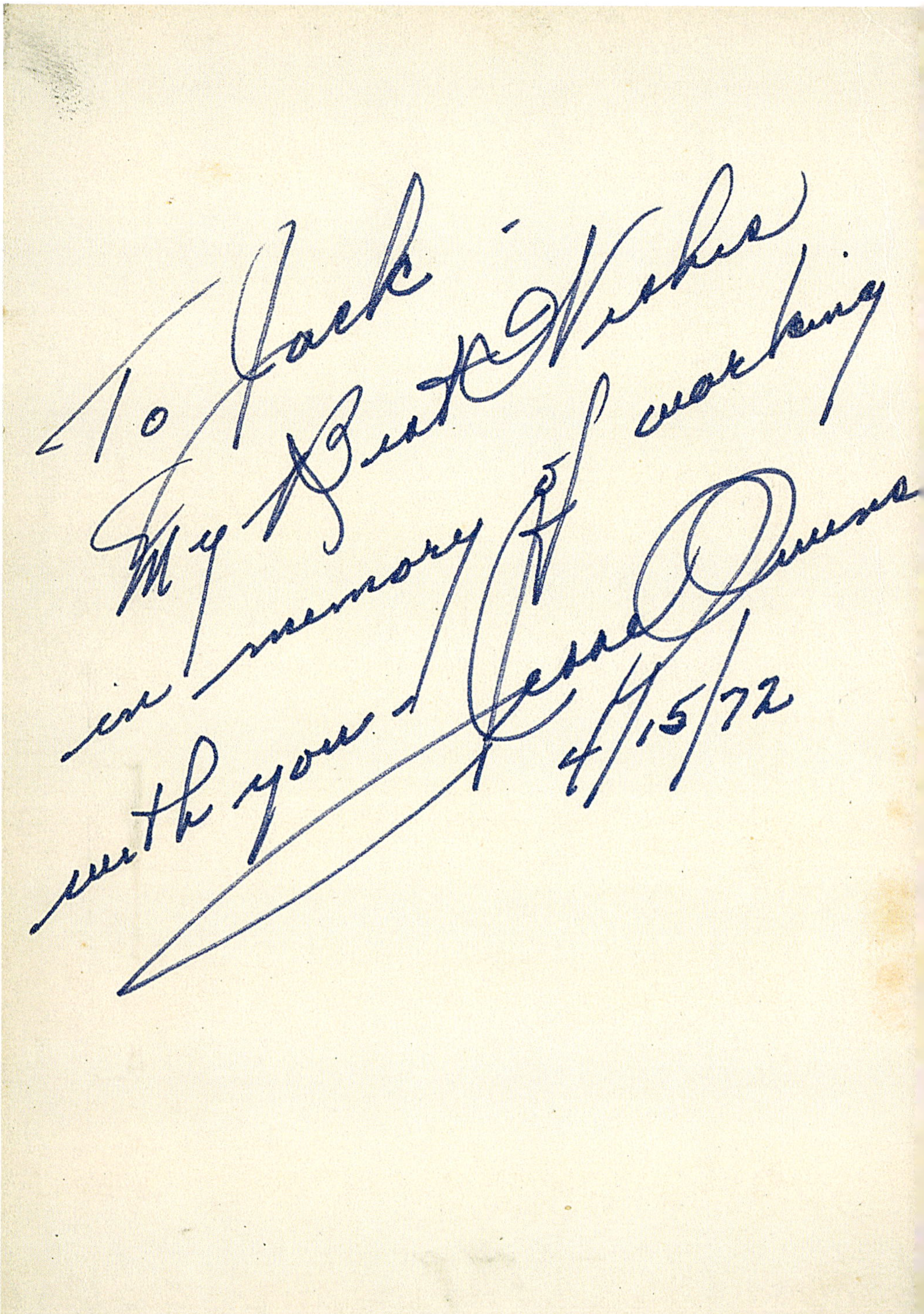
To Jack
My Best Wishes
in memory of working
with you. Jesse Owens
4/15/72

Jesse Owens and Jack

C-COR

OLYMPIC SERIES
a real champion

The course took place in the Pennsylvania mountain wilderness and incorporated lessons of leadership and Scouting discipline that future Scout leaders could bring back to their Scout troops. Jack was elected patrol leader for his adult patrol group, and he enjoyed the experience very much.

All three of Jack's sons, John, Peter, and Jim, achieved the highly respected rank of Eagle Scout. John and Pete both made Eagle Scout in the late 1960s while at Troop 380 in Boalsburg, Pennsylvania. Jim received the honor in 1972 at Troop 83 in State College, at the very young age of thirteen. Becoming Eagle Scout required that the boys advance through several ranks, earn numerous required merit badges, complete a meaningful public-service project, and exemplify the principles of the Boy Scout oath. Only 4% of Scouts achieve the rank.

Jack Ingram knew that young men needed guidance, and he was one of the best natural-born counselors. Never did he call the boys "kids" even though they were very young. He always challenged them to step up, think through challenges, and turn them into opportunities. Jack was a firm believer in the statement, "Better done than said!" He believed in a "can-do" attitude, teaching the boys how to lead through the examples he set. Bonnie Glen served as a great backdrop for numerous Scout troop camping trips, creating memories for dozens of young men growing up in State College.

Being a Boy Scout taught young men to be prepared, not unlike soldiers or seamen. Jack's entire life, from his time on the Rogue River, through his military and intelligence service, into his retirement work, Jack adapted to constant change and overcame hurdles in his path. He taught dozens of young Scouts to do the same.

Jack's fifteenth great leadership character trait was *resilience*!

Chapter Sixteen

Everyone's Dad

Jack kept busy with his various post-retirement jobs and volunteer work, and he was now able to spend more time with his family. With an age spread of more than twenty years, it seemed as though Jack and Doris's children were involved with every activity imaginable. And all of them were growing up so fast! During the early 1960s, Jack took an art class at Penn State with his daughter, Beverly. They were featured as a father-daughter team taking the course in an article in the State College newspaper, *Centre Daily Times*. Art became a lifelong passion the two of them shared.

On the 24th of September 1965, Karen married John Martin Horvath. Coincidentally, John was another young man who had been handpicked by the NSA. He had been assigned to oversee quality control and daily security protocols for top-secret projects at HRB-Singer. Years later, John would go on to champion NSA work for more than forty years. He would retire from the NSA before the 9/11 attack but would return afterward. Karen became known as an excellent teacher in the Baltimore-Washington area and she would become a dynamic Catholic high school principal in McLean, Virginia, eventually retiring to help her own children with their growing families. Together, Karen and John would raise five children; John, Julie, Christie, Kathleen, and Marita.

A year later, Beverly married William Joseph Klucher, Jr., on the 18th of September 1966. Bill was a brilliant engineer who worked on top-secret projects at HRB-Singer as well. He was one of the few young engineers selected by Boeing to help expedite the space race. He also worked on government projects that he could never talk about. As an engineering "job shopper," he later worked on a project to design the first moon pack for astronauts, as well as the SR-71 Blackbird spy plane—at that time, the fastest plane ever built!

After starting a family, Bev returned to Penn State full time and graduated with a Bachelor of Fine Arts. For many years, Bev taught and mentored local artists, becoming well known as one of the best oil painters in the central Pennsylvania region. Landscapes, seascapes, portraits, and religious subjects highlighted her diverse abilities. She even painted a portrait of Pope John Paul II that she personally delivered to Rome. Together, Bev and Bill would raise two children, Bill and Jeanne.

John graduated from Penn State with a double B.A. in geography and political science in June 1971. Later, John served two years in the U.S. Army, stationed in Washington, D.C., assigned to locate soldiers who had gone absent without official leave (AWOL) during our involvement in the Vietnam War. John's ability to use early computers and interact with people who were not so willing to give up information made him uniquely qualified for such a duty. After serving in the army, he went back to school and earned his Master of Urban and Regional Planning from Rutgers University, qualifying him to work with regional government plans around the country. John also had a brief stint working on Wall Street for Merrill Lynch and later on government projects. He decided to attain his Member Appraisal Institute (MAI) appraisal designation, encouraging him to start his own successful real estate appraisal company. John had two children, Peter and Roxanne.

Jim would go on to graduate from forestry school at Penn State Mont Alto. After working at the Penn State University Forest Resources Lab in genetics research, he would return to school to receive another degree in agriculture. He worked his way through school counseling in the dorms. Later he would teach forestry and counseling at Mont Alto and eventually work for the best private tree-care provider in the world: Bartlett Tree Experts. Moving to Cape Cod, he would marry Barbara Graeff from Shillington, Pennsylvania. Barb graduated from Penn State in business management, where they met. Barb and Jim would raise Jack and Sage on the Cape where the trees meet the sea.

During the early 1970s, young Mary Etta was playing the flute and attending grade school at Our Lady of Victory Catholic School. She grew up and married John Jeske, a skilled carpenter. Mary Etta became an art teacher, continuing to work with her natural artistic abilities in the Columbia, Maryland, region. Mary Etta and John had three children, Philip, Joseph, and Maria.

Peter Ingram

By March of 1973, Jack had become well known for his ability to give speeches to interested groups at Penn State and around Pennsylvania. For some time, he gave interviews on radio shows in State College about the Great Depression of the 1930s—placer mining for gold on the Rogue River—and his navy experiences before, during, and after WWII.

To honor his sworn secrecy to the nation, he never spoke on radio shows about his major responsibilities as a government agent and trainer attached to national security agencies. He limited his navy talks to his other duties and experiences on ships. He talked about his time aboard USS *Pennsylvania*, biplane operations, being a member of the "Hindenburg Class," setting up weather stations for the Pacific fleet, WWII bombing missions over Japan, and hurricane hunting in Miami. He also talked about more recent duties on USS *Ranger* and jet aircraft operations.

As with most families, life held some tragedies for Jack Ingram's family. Bad news arrived on October 22, 1974, when they lost Peter Allen. He was shot with a rifle in a terrible incident, and after a short three-day investigation the police proclaimed it to be a "self-inflicted gunshot wound." Jack asked, "How could it be self-inflicted if the gun was on the other side of the room from where they found Pete?"

Peter was buried at Graysville Cemetery west of State College. It was a horrifying time for the entire Ingram family. Pete had been a Penn State landscape architect and art education student who had been president of his Kappa Delta Rho fraternity. He was athletic and was a charismatic mentor to his younger brother, Jim, and to the other Boy Scouts in their troop. As an Eagle Scout, he proved himself to be a master of the Bonnie Glen wilderness. He was bright and outgoing and made friends quickly.

For months, mystery surrounded Pete's movements and interactions leading up to his death. Without any help from the police, Jack initiated his own thorough investigation that illuminated Pete's involvement in drug trade from Florida to New York City, Philadelphia, and State College. Jack's background in intelligence gathering and documentation enabled him to assemble a complete chronology and substantiation of Pete's drug trafficking as well as to provide the names of others who had been involved leading up to his last day.

In the process, Jack also learned whom Pete had alienated. Through personal interviews and documentation, Jack found out that Pete had decided to get out of the business three months before he was killed. It became apparent that Pete had turned on people in the drug trade because of their poor treatment, in some cases murder, of his friends. Jack deduced that the drug traffickers were threatened and scared that Pete would expose them!

One evening, with Pete's brother, Jim, along, Jack met with local police authorities, showing them evidence about several people who could be responsible for Pete's shooting. Even though there was overwhelming evidence regarding possible perpetrators, and Jack's legal-style brief was very clear and concise, the local police were not interested in any further investigation. Regardless of the evidence, they did not want to hear the facts or about the possibility of revenge and murder. Jack began to suspect that they were protecting either themselves or other people. There was a turning point in the conversation at which Jack knew to refrain, and he artfully deescalated their fear. Jack was an astute student of human behavior. He was a master at reading people, and he knew he had to convince the authorities to believe that he was going to leave the situation alone.

Jack, now concerned that his family could be threatened if he pursued the case, made Jim promise that he would never discuss the outcome of the police meeting with his mother, the family, or anyone else. He was afraid for their safety. Jim had never seen such anger and fear in his father's eyes. To watch him stand down when he knew that he was right really tore Jim up inside. How could he could ignore such pain and anger? The incident ultimately gave Jim a new perspective on his father's capacity for restraint and his ability to internalize such devastating things.

In November of 1974, Jack stopped working for anyone else—including the government. Jack and Doris started making plans to move out of State College to Bonnie Glen full time because it had become very difficult for the family to remain in town given the vivid memories of Peter.

In the summer of 1975 the family moved to their country home that had been built in 1830, Bonnie Glen. The entire family pitched in to help with the move, as well as with improvements to the old house. The two youngest children, Jim and Mary Etta, transferred into much smaller classes in the Penns Valley School District, twenty miles away.

Bonnie Glen would become a well-deserved refuge for the Ingram family. It offered a peaceful place to reflect on the good times of the past and to renew their spirits going forward. The mountains, forests, springs, streams, and wildlife through the changing seasons allowed them to heal from the tragic and sudden shock of losing Pete.

Jack knew that Jim was especially drawn to the trees and the wilderness environment on the property and over the mountain in the neighboring mountain forests. He would sometimes venture out for days at a time! It seemed that Jack's son had inherited the love of the outdoors that Jack had gained during his time on the Rogue River.

In the spring of 1976, as a high school junior, Jim inquired about the Naval Academy and recruiters were knocking on the door suggesting that his passion for trees and forests could be satisfied by taking the U.S. Marine route, specializing in forest photo interpretation and intelligence. Jim, having acquired the local congressman's nod to go, thought he would really make his father proud.

But one spring day, Jack asked, "What the hell do you want to go into the navy for—trees don't grow at sea!" Jack had done his homework and the next day he drove Jim two and a half hours to Penn State Mont Alto. It was a top forestry school dedicated to teaching the art and science of forest management. The school dated back to 1903 and some of its first graduates opened the new national forest lands in the western states for Teddy Roosevelt and Gifford Pinchot back in the early 1900s. Jim and Jack were able to visit the school and see the curriculum and opportunities.

On the way home, Jack said, "So, Jim, what did you think?"

Jim replied enthusiastically, "It's great!"

Jack asked, "Do you think you want to go there?"

"Absolutely!"

He quickly added, "Well, you'll still have to pay your own way—I'm sure you'll figure it out."

In June 1978, Jack and Doris arranged to fly back to their home state of Oregon for a visit. It would be the first visit ever for Jim and Mary Etta, and it had been thirty years since Jack and Doris uprooted and left their families. The trip included visiting relatives, friends, and various parts of the Pacific Northwest from Portland and Seattle to southern Oregon and northern California and back to Portland. In all, they were gone for thirty days.

One special day was spent retracing the footsteps of Jack and his father, Earl, on the Rogue River to their gold claim at Ennis Riffle near Galice. They found the old campsite where they once placer mined for gold. As he stood on the bank of the river, Jack recalled, "Shoveling pay dirt is not all it's cracked up to be, especially in this box canyon with temperatures that would get over 100 by two o'clock in the afternoon."

For Jim, the entire trip took on special meaning. He'd spent many a wonderful day with his dad in the wilderness at Bonnie Glen, listening to stories about the days on the Rogue River. Jim admired the life his father had growing up, surviving the hard times, living off the land, and being self-sufficient.

"Dad, I remember you telling me stories about an old Spanish-American War veteran, Crowe, who lived in a cabin a quarter mile down the river. Remember? He used to tell you stories of his life and adventures in the West?"

"Remember?" Jack responded. "It seems like just yesterday to me. What do you say we hike down the river trail to see if his old cabin still exists?"

"Can we?" Jim was already heading down the river as he responded. He was already living a great adventure!

As father and son approached the area, they saw that not only did the cabin still exist, but there was an old guy there splitting and stacking wood!!

In Jack's forthright fashion, he walked up to the elderly gentleman, extended his hand, and introduced himself, "Hello, my name is Jack Ingram, and this is my son, Jim. I lived on the river in the thirties with my dad."

The gentleman smiled, shook Jack's hand, looked him square in the eye, and said, "You're the young punk that used to screw up my fishing! I'm Fly—Remember? I fished for steelhead and you used to swim right in front of my line! You and your dad had many a dinner with me at your camp and here at Crowe's cabin."

Mr. Fly had been a wealthy recreational fly-fisherman who had befriended Earl and Jack many years before. It did not take long for the two men to renew their bond as they rekindled stories of the Rogue.

Jack's last professional photo

Jim could hardly believe any of this was happening. It seemed like the stories his father had told him for years were coming true right before his eyes. As Jack and his son headed back up the river to rejoin Doris and Mary Etta, Jim did not want the moment to end.

Finally, the Ingram family's adventure was winding down. They went down to the Oregon Caves, crossed the border into northern California to enjoy the huge Redwood trees, and then headed back north along coast to the former site of Wecoma, where Jack and Doris had spent their one-week honeymoon in November of 1941. Wecoma had been swallowed up and merged with four other cities to become Lincoln City, so it was difficult to find the precise cottage, but they did! It was a nostalgic time for Jack and Doris. Eventually, they all returned to Jack's sister Mary's house in Portland for a big dinner before flying back to Bonnie Glen.

In 1979, John Richard Ingram II announced his engagement to Ms. Rose Sgarlata of Brooklyn, New York. They were married on May 18 at Regina Pacis Shrine by Father Bob who also administered the nuptial blessing at the wedding. Jim was best man, Mary Etta was a bridesmaid, and all the family attended.

Jack spoke often of his adventures in life, especially his time in the navy. Often he was asked the same question, "How could you stand twenty-eight years of navy life?"

Jack's succinct philosophy summed it all up. "I can give you four excellent reasons!" Jack would respond.

"Number 1: I had my own private yacht complete with qualified crew.

"Number 2: I always had a band, horns, and a welcome home ceremony.

"Number 3: I had no expenses for sightseeing the world, with pay to boot.And

"Number 4: I could send a message anytime, anywhere in the world—almost."

Jack enjoyed passing along what he had learned at each stage of his life, not only to his children but also to many others. Eventually, each of his children could recite their favorite stories almost word for word. But Jim was always the most enamored of all. He revered his father and hoped to make him proud someday.

One cool, bright autumn day, September 16, 1980, Jack and Doris drove down to visit Jim at Penn State's main campus in State College. Jim had gone back to school to get another degree. He was a counselor in the dorms and working at the forest genetics lab to pay for school. At one point, Jack got up and started looking around Jim's dorm room at the awards and memorabilia he had acquired over the years. He said, "Wow, I never knew you had done so many things, Jim."

Jim said right back to him, "Dad, you accomplished a lot more than me by the time you were 21!"

The afternoon progressed as they all talked about their latest activities and news. Eventually it was time for Jim to join his buddies for an intramural football game. Jack and Doris decided to do a little shopping at Weis Markets in town before heading back to Bonnie Glen.

Shortly after venturing off to the market, Jack suffered a massive heart attack and died.

The family was stunned. Somehow Jack had always seemed invincible. It was like everyone expected he would live forever.

In some ways he did. Jack lived on in his stories and his legacy. Jack Ingram's story is of a boy who grew up with very little but who had everything important. It is the story of how the U.S. Navy gave birth to an officer with "unlimited duty." It is the chronicle of how a young man from Oregon, with limited resources, gifted his leadership to everyone he encountered. Jack believed, and he made no secret of his belief, that a good person must also be a good citizen. He excelled at being both a good person and a good citizen, with his success helping family, friends, and country.

Jack was a man of high morals, a man who lived his life with integrity.

Jack's sixteenth great leadership character trait was *integrity*!

Chapter Seventeen
Practical Reflections

In reflecting about Jack's life, I think about his start. He was a survivor of the Great Depression and WWII, and his deep faith was central to his way of life and embedded in everything he encountered. A son of a Baptist father and Catholic mother, he possessed a great penchant for sacrificing in order to help his family, his country, and others.

Jack was born in 1917 in Portland, a short distance from Verboort, Oregon, where his maternal grandparents, Peter and Johanna Jansen, had cultivated their Willamette Valley farm. Since 1871, the Jansens had been part of a small hardworking Dutch-Catholic colony of six families from De Pere, Wisconsin, that were drawn west, like so many families, by the promise of Oregon's rich forests and farm land. Good soil was vital to pioneer farming families!

Father William Verboort, who was a missionary priest, guided the Dutch families from Wisconsin to Oregon. Father Verboort died less than a year after they arrived at the young age of forty, and the settlers named the community after him. Father Verboort's spirit and vision to build a church and set up a community to perpetuate their faith and farming enterprise continued on in the Dutch settlers, and inevitably their beliefs and devotion were carried down to Jack Ingram.

During numerous summers on the Jansen farm, Jack was deeply imprinted by the Catholic religion of his mother's family. His grandparents, aunts, uncles, and cousins were of modest means but were highly respected for their kindness and commitment to each other and their small community. Every summer became dearer to him than the last, as Jack learned what his faith meant to him. In turn, he would show others goodness through his deeds, where acts of kindness were better done than said. It is remarkable to know that, over his summers on the farm, Jack acquired the rudiments of his lifelong faith.

Later in life, both Jack and Doris would teach their three boys and three girls the importance of maintaining a strong faith through service to others. Jack would explain how faith helped to guide him through many of life's trials. From losing his mother at a very young age to the adversities he encountered during the Depression and WWII, Jack would describe how he would restore his spirit by using the power of self-reflection and prayer.

Throughout his entire navy career, Jack befriended chaplains who helped guide both his spiritual and military life before, during, and after WWII. Father Charles E. Deppermann, director of the Manila Observatory and the world's foremost authority on typhoons, wrote to Commander Lockhart saying, "Jack is a good aerographer friend of mine, and I want you to give him some sound advice as to how he can further his career as an aerographer. He is ambitious to advance, and I believe he has the stuff in him to do it if rightly guided." Jack learned a lot about faith and meteorology from Deppermann. Fascinatingly, MacArthur's paratroops rescued Deppermann from Japanese imprisonment and he was flown to Washington, D.C., to assist in planning for an invasion of the Japanese homeland that never happened.

Jack's faith was never stronger than when it came to help his hometown parish Catholic Church. He loved to serve on building committees. He enjoyed working with his fellow parishioners to realize their collective hopes and dreams by helping to oversee church construction projects from St. John's Church in McLean, Virginia, Our Lady of Victory Church in State College, Pennsylvania, to St. Kateri Tekakwitha Church in Spring Mills, Pennsylvania. He was the most comfortable when his volunteer time meant achieving a clear and compelling goal that served as a focal point for faith.

Jack's early boyhood lessons of faith were alive and well throughout his entire life. He had an innate quality of helping people feel that any tough experience could be overcome with a little faith.

In Jack's personal papers, we found the following quote, "In order to live happily in the community, and to labor effectively for the attainment of satisfaction, we must endure much, and restrain ourselves upon many occasions. As the dispositions of those with whom we live are often contrary to our own, humility and grace must preserve peace and charity, by enabling us to suffer and to bear controversy, as nature preserves the order of all things by reconciling a contrariety of the elements."

Jack's seventeenth great leadership character trait was *enduring faith*!

Author's Notes

Sage Advice

Researching and writing this book has been an incredible journey for me. In retrospect, I knew my dad as a loving person who always wanted to help us to safely navigate the waters of life. Many of his stories were lessons so that we would never have to endure certain avoidable pains of life.

As far back as I can remember, there were always stories—stories of World War II, stories of flying though hurricanes, stories of travel to exotic places, and my favorite, stories of life on the Rogue River. The opportunity to return there with my father was, for me, surreal. All of his stories suddenly came to life and I felt as though I was there with him.

One of his favorite topics was his personal role in helping people during the Hindenburg disaster. In 1937, his assignment along with the rest of the landing crew was to hold down the landing lines. His position on the lines was where the con cabin would come to rest. There were rousing cheers as the great airship settled toward its mooring. Then the loud shocking boom and the radio announcer yelling, "Run for your life!"

I will never forget a trip we took to Cape May on the Jersey shore in the early 1970s. Dad decided to make a detour to show Mom, Mary Etta, and me Lakehurst Naval Air Station. As we drove up to Lakehurst's main gate, a young marine guard asked Dad about his business. From behind several other ID cards in his wallet, Dad pulled his military ID out for the marine and said, "I thought I'd show the family around."

The marine took one look at Dad's ID, stood at attention, saluted Dad, and said, "Yes sir!" He then politely requested that we park off to the side of the building in a special parking area. I could not have been prouder of my father at that moment.

A few minutes later, a navy officer drove up to the gate with another younger sailor. My dad got out of our car and started to speak with the air station's commander who gladly decided to come out and greet Dad and the rest of us. He asked Dad to follow him to his office. The officer gave us refreshments and Dad proceeded to tell the Hindenburg story and many other side stories about his aerography class and Lakehurst history of the 1930s. The CO and two other navy personnel gave us a grand tour of the base, including a walk all around the site where the dirigible went down and the huge circular rail to which the ground crew was supposed to tie the tail of the airship after it had been secured to the mooring mast. Dad proclaimed, "The Hindenburg was the world's largest weather vane."

I could not believe the magnitude of the old dirigible hanger and how it dwarfed the jets that were parked inside. The day turned out to be one that would validate every one of my dad's stories!

Now, Dad could do some storytelling, and the Aleutian campaign was another favorite. This was where the navy men coined the phrase, "Never a sailor will you be until you've sailed the Bering Sea." Dad's notes include such personal quips as his joy in getting fresh milk from the "gifted cow."

Then there were his travels in the peacetime navy to the Far East. Whenever I would watch WWII movies, I'd recognize the names of the places, and it would make the stories more real for me. He spoke of his experience of "rounding the Horn" on USS *Ranger* in June of 1958. He visited parts of the world as a young man that few of us ever will.

Hurricane hunting was always an exciting topic too, and one Dad also covered during radio interviews. Most of us would not fly into the eye of a hurricane for a million dollars, but Dad did it many times, and in 1940s airplanes! There were so many different facets to this remarkable man. He lived a life that never seemed to have a dull moment, leaving behind a legacy that the entire family continues to honor and cherish to this day.

I remember vividly the cool, bright autumn day of September 16, 1980. The day started out as another day of new classes at Penn State's main campus in State College. I had gone back to school to get another degree and Dad and Mom came from Bonnie Glen to visit with me in my dorm, East

Halls. I was still a counselor in the dorms and working at the forest genetics lab to pay for school. I also had started to work out with the track team. On that afternoon, I was dressing to play in an intermural football game with my dorm buddies when my parents dropped by to see me.

I'll never forget talking with Dad and Mom that afternoon. I couldn't believe it when Dad started talking about *my* accomplishments. How could my life ever compare to his? Nevertheless, it meant so much to me to feel his pride.

When I said goodbye to them, I had no idea that these would be the last words I'd ever speak to my father. After the football game, I was told that Dad had suffered a massive heart attack and died shortly after leaving campus.

For me, the world stood still.

I sprinted to be with my mom at my sister Bev's house on Saxton Drive, State College, remembering the words of wisdom my dad had told me when my brother died, "Jim, you need to be strong and try to help everyone else during these times of sorrow." It was easier said than done!

Jack Ingram was incredibly service oriented, not just in the military, but in everyday life with the people around him. Whether he was helping young men in the Boy Scouts to become good members of their community or helping young professionals understand their roles in positively affecting society, Dad always took the time to listen to everyone's hopes, dreams, and desires. He also made a point of doing what he called, "a good turn for the day." He would help someone with the simplest of things and then say, "That's my good turn for the day."

My father was instrumental in my career choice. He recognized my passion for trees and the outdoors, and he steered me away from the navy. Thanks to him, I enrolled in a fantastic forestry curriculum in 1977 at Penn State Mont Alto, excelling in all my scientific and technical courses. And I found a way to pay for my education by agreeing to become a counselor in the dorms that paid all my room and board plus half of the tuition. In 1979, I graduated from Penn State Mont Alto with a forestry degree. I was fortunate to win the first Pennsylvania State Forest

Academy Award at graduation—and I dedicated it to Dad, with him in attendance, because of his vision regarding my true professional passion. I am glad there was an opportunity to do such a thing because Dad never looked for any acknowledgement for his personal professional career. It was my good turn for the day!

There is one last story I will never forget about my dad. At the time, I was a young man and I was doing well. I was teaching forestry and counseling at Penn State Mont Alto, and I had agreed that day to join Bartlett Tree Experts in Bala Cynwyd, Pennsylvania. I just bought a new car and that was a big deal to me—getting a loan from the bank and the whole nine yards.

Driving home to see my mom in Woodward, a two-and-a-half-hour drive, I was on the highway and I was really testing this car out—seeing what it's got—when I got stopped by a Pennsylvania state trooper. He came up to my car, looked at my license, looked at me, looked back at the license, looked at me again, and then he said, "You know something? If your dad knew that you were speeding the way you just were, going home to see your mom, he'd be really upset with you. Because you've got to be there for your mom."

I was thinking, *Who is this guy?* And I said, "Yeah, you're right. How did you know?"

And he answered, "Oh, I've heard all about you through the years. I used to be a security guard at the company that your dad consulted for, HRB, and at the end of the day he'd come down and ask me how I was doing. He'd spend sometimes twenty minutes talking to me about life, and you were a big piece of that."

"We'd talk about what I should do with my life. He knew that I wanted to be a state trooper, and he told me that I had to follow my dream. He wrote me a recommendation. And he said, 'That is just one piece, one step at a time.' He gave me confidence, and he's the reason I became a state trooper and left that security desk at HRB."

"So," he said, "What I'm going to do is, if you promise to me that you're not going to be conducting yourself like this on the highway again, I'll let you go without a ticket to go see your mom, because your mom is really important. And, it's great to see you!"

Jack Ingram had great influence on people. It was not about money. It was not about ego. It was about one person at a time. And, he took the time with everyone, helping them to navigate in the world!

To this day, my fellow Boy Scouts who knew my dad share how much he influenced their lives and how, with his words of wisdom and his genuine interest in their well-being, he positively impacted their lives. Through his stories and practical lessons, we all learned the basic tenets of leadership.

The conclusions I have reached about dad's life are based on what I have heard, lived, seen, and known—all of which I had to share. Dad's leadership traits—self-worth, humility, bravery, loyalty, stability, inspiration, confidence, respect, friendship, introspection, courage, insight, confidentiality, dedication, resilience, integrity, and enduring faith—all buoyed his application of common sense to common problems for the common good.

And that is far from the whole story. What people knew about Dad concentrated on what he could discuss; it never included his classified intelligence work. How far he was willing to go in pursuit of protecting the country has been shown throughout his navy career and beyond. That is as much as we have known about. Personal profit was never put before patriotism!

Jack could not foretell just what impact he would have on his family or country. At each turning point in his life, two great human forces motivated him to do the right thing. One demanded him to survive and prosper for his family. The other drove him to serve our country. Combined, these forces, for the most part, kept his family and country safe at all costs!

Over many years, my dad told me vivid stories and gave me invaluable, sage advice. Jack Ingram always inspired people to lead by turning challenges into success, so that they could teach others to do the same. I only hope that I can do him service, by sharing his stories, lessons, and advice with my own family and with the people around me.

Afterword

Jack Ingram by Ken Schmidt

I find it telling that, of the thousands of people I've met, worked with and befriended over my lifetime, there are just a handful of folks I remember well enough from my formative days to be able to share stories about them. The common thread running through these folks is the fact that each of them made the kind of extraordinary contributions to my life that, even as a kid, I knew set them apart from others. That's why they're remembered. Sports coaches—the volunteer kind—and a few teachers stand out in my mind. As does, at the top of the list, Jack Ingram.

I later served as a scout volunteer for my son's troop—the die to be involved with kids, undoubtedly, was cast by Jack. I always taught the young scout leaders something Jack taught me that took me by surprise, as it always did to others when I shared it. As I'd grown to be one of our troop's "patrol leaders," I'd organized a game of softball to cap off a weekend camping trip. After a few innings, Jack pulled me aside and said, "Wrap up the game now, Ken." I protested, "Why now? We've having a blast!" He said, "That's exactly why you should end it now. Let their last memory of the camp-out be how much fun they're having, so they'll want to come again next time and bring some friends with them." That's solid gold. And it works every time, even in my professional life.

I was oddly delighted to see in Jim's book some of Jack's poems, as they illuminated a memory I've carried forever. At one of my earliest scout meetings, in a frigid cold metal storage garage (barely heated by a wood-burning stove) behind the church that sponsored Troop 83, Jack challenged us kids to write a poem about our excitement that spring was approaching. At our next troop meeting, Jack read some of the poems out loud and, I clearly recall, was very excited about it. When he read mine, the older kids laughed and ribbed me, but Jack was having none of it. "You know why you guys are laughing?" he asked. "It's because you know this is very good and you're wishing you'd taken the time to do such a nice job." Learning of his love for poetry—which I found surprising, given the rugged, "manly" nature of his life—I now see not only why he gave us that assignment, but why he took it so seriously. Who remembers writing a poem 50 years ago? And what it was about? I do.

Like Jack, my father, and fathers of many of my childhood friends, worked in the defense industry and thus, were extremely tight-lipped about everything and everyone. I assumed all adults were like this and that nobody ever talked about their work, but of course, have long since learned that I was wrong. Despite never naming names or specifics, my dad always said, "Jack Ingram's the real deal." Meaning, there was something extra special about him.

The Ingrams were neighbors when I was growing up, and everyone in my family knew them well. My brothers and I knew that Jack led the local Scout troop and, based on stories we'd heard about it from "older boys," were very eager to grow old enough to join. What I knew as a ten-year old of camping and outdoor skills, let alone leadership or self-organization, could fit into a thimble, but that was to change quickly for me and my brothers. To this day—50 years later!—we often quote Jack Ingram when we're together fishing and camping, as he's the one who ushered us into nature in the first place. When building a fire, we'll all say, "Punk don't burn, son! Punk don't burn!" meaning, "Go find some dry kindling!" We've all said that hundreds of times. The use of flashlights in the woods is something we simply don't do. Why? Because Jack told us, "Turn that off! You'll scare whatever's here. Let your eyes adjust. You can see a lot more than you think you can." Simple stuff, to be sure. Yet remembered. Word-for-word. And all because a man who lived for others wanted to pass on his knowledge (as so, too, have my brothers and I).

To read that Jack had such a remarkable, rich past only adds to the esteem in which I hold him. That he kept it to himself is understandable, but I'm so glad Jim worked long and hard to bring Jack's stories to life, as they certainly deserve to be known and recognized. As a WWII history buff, I'll not be able to think of that "greatest generation" without thinking foremost of Jack Ingram. He was, without question, a man for others and a man to be admired. I'm glad to know him so much better now. I love this book!

We all knew Jack was a master of the outdoor world and that he very clearly enjoyed sharing his knowledge with us. The camp-outs of my youth—and I know I share this in common with the other guys who were there—are among the best memories of my life. Jack never preached or got in the way. Instead he patiently instructed and offered tons of encouragement. No kid, ever, was left out or mocked, and no kid didn't light up on getting compliments from Jack. Our campfires were epic nights of skits and singing (imagine that), and I have to wonder how awestruck we'd have been if Jack had shared some tales of his incredible past. What kid wouldn't get bug-eyed hearing about the *Hindenberg* explosion? Or of WWII battles in the Pacific? Or fishing the Rogue and prospecting for gold? Nope.

Jack made everything about us, sat back, enjoyed the camaraderie and chewed his ever-present pipe. I guarantee every kid who ever witnessed this over Jack's many years as Scoutmaster can picture him in the firelight, because that image of what a "real man" looks like is seared into our memory banks. We knew so few like him.

Ken Schmidt, the legendary Director of Communications at Harley-Davidson Motor Company, is the author of *Make Some Noise.*

rthwest at 8.7 knots.

	WEATHER FORECAST	WEATHER OBSERVED
Y	Cloudy	Cloudy to overcast
EATHER	Scattered showers	Scattered showers
SIBILITY	10 miles	10 - 15 miles
ND	West 6 - 13 knots	West-Northwest 7 - 10 knots
A	Slight (Increasing)	Slight

SUPPLEMENTARY INFORMATION

Barometer 1006.0 millibars (29.71 inches)

Base of low clouds, Estimated 2500 feet.

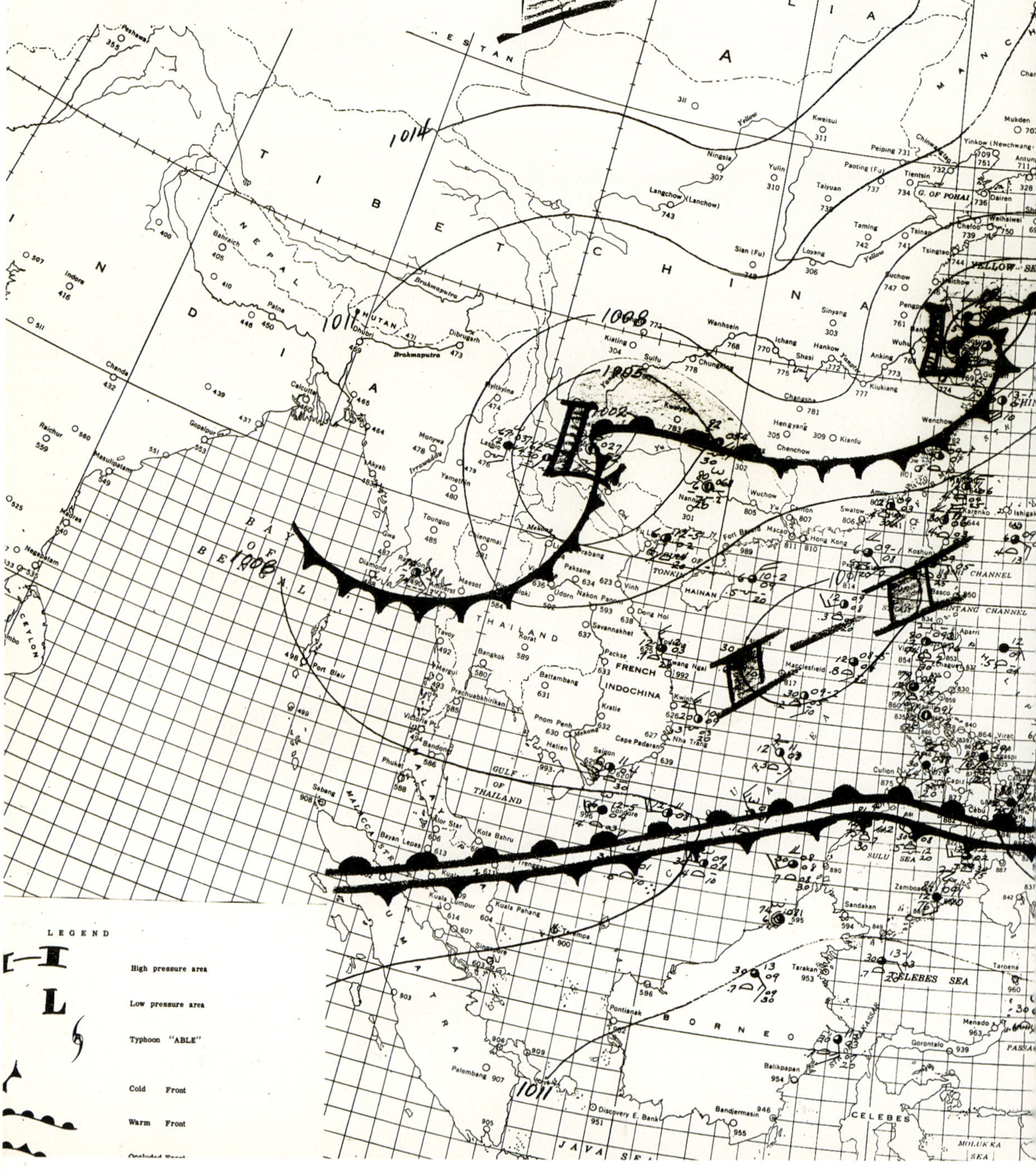